SUISUN VALLEY SCHOOL

SUISUN VALLEY SCHOOL
FSUSD

S0-BNJ-717

THE MYSTERY OF THE FLOODED MINE

Doubleday Signal Books

THE MYSTERY OF
THE FLOODED MINE

by Willard Manus

ILLUSTRATED BY
James Dwyer

Doubleday & Company, Inc.
Garden City, New York

Library of Congress Catalog Card Number 64–13844
Copyright © 1964 by Doubleday & Company, Inc.
All Rights Reserved
Printed in the United States of America

Prepared by Rutledge Books

SUISUN VALLEY SCHOOL LIBRARY
FSUSD

Contents

85130

Chapter 1

A LONG WAY FROM THE SEA

I had been driving since dawn, and I was hot, tired and hungry. My rattly jeep, which I had bought at a used-car lot just a few days before, was beginning to overheat as it toiled up the winding mountain road.

I was not used to mountains. I am a skin diver by profession—Bill Bryan is my name—and my home is the sea. Then what was I doing way up there in the mountains? I was planning to dive for gold.

I suppose it sounds crazy. Well, I was beginning to think so myself.

As I took a long curve, I came on a small lake. I blinked hard, thinking the sun was playing tricks with my eyes. But it was there all right—a small circle of icy blue water.

I pulled off the road and parked in the shade of two

big trees, where I took out my lunch box and opened my jar of coffee. While I ate, I read for the tenth time the letter from my old skin-diving pal, Arnie Lewis:

"Dear Bill:

"By the time you get this, I will have quit the California mountains and the under-water search for gold.

"As you know, I was very excited when I first came here. There were several of us on the project. It was fun hunting for gold and having some sport at the same time. But now a new kind of skin diver has come in.

"These men have all the equipment, and they dive, but they are different. They don't care a hoot for the sport, and they refuse to help one another. Many of them will do anything to get their hands on gold—lie, cheat, steal, maybe even kill.

"I've had it! My group has broken up and I'm going to New York. I know I urged you to join our search for gold, but now I advise you to stay out."

I stared down at the letter. If only it had come a week ago, before I had spent my last cent on the jeep and all this equipment! Now I *had* to search for gold.

I had not believed, at first, that you could dive for gold. Then, about six months ago, Arnie went off in to the mountains, and I began to get letters from him, telling about the fortunes some of his friends were making.

"Come on and join us, Bill," he wrote then. "The old mines are paying off again."

I knew something of the old mines. A hundred years ago, there had been a great gold rush in California. Thousands of men had poured in to the mountains hoping to strike it rich. Some did. Great fortunes were made. Deep shafts were dug in the earth by men who went down and hacked out vast amounts of gold. Others waded into rivers and streams, and sifted with pans and screens for the precious yellow dust.

The boom came to an end almost as suddenly as it had begun. Rivers ran dry, mines became worked out. The new miners seeking gold became desperate. They blasted deeper in to the earth. They threw up dams and tried to change the direction of rivers. But all they did was flood the mine shafts with ice-cold waters. After that, no one could mine, and the men pulled out and went home. The whole bustling, noisy country suddenly fell silent. The great gold rush was over. Nature again took over the hills, and peace returned to the land.

It remained that way for 110 years—until some skin divers showed up one day, searching for new waters to explore. They were in search of sport, not gold. But in the course of their exploring, they came across gold nuggets lodged in the cracks of river shallows. The word "gold" was heard in California again.

That started it. Immediately divers began to flock to these hills, my friend Arnie among them. When he first wrote, urging me to come and join him, I laughed it off. But later I began to see it another way. I was out of work for the moment, and this seemed like a good chance for adventure.

Then, as I was ready to set out, the letter had come, warning me of trouble.

It did not seem possible that these empty mountains, dotted with pine trees, could be dangerous. But Arnie was no coward—if he said to watch out, then there was something to watch out for.

Far away, on the other side of the lake, I noticed something moving. I reached down and picked up my field glasses. They brought in to view several wooden shacks and two tents. It looked like a permanent camp there on the far side of the lake.

My glasses made out a young boy—maybe 15 or 16—and an old man with a white beard. They were standing side by side, peering out over the lake. I turned my glasses in the direction they were looking and spotted a man swimming toward the shore. He was wearing a face mask and had air tanks strapped to his back. He was moving in a crippled way as though in pain.

I shot a look at the shore. The boy had thrown himself in to the water and was swimming furiously toward the man. I was not sure what was wrong, but I knew I had better get there fast.

I raced the jeep down the side of the hill and roared along the edge of the lake, skidding where it was soft and wet. I was thankful for the jeep, which could shoot over this kind of ground with ease. Stones flew up and rattled against the under side, but I made it to the camp seconds later.

Out in the lake the boy was yelling, "Dad! Dad!"

"What happened?" I shouted at the old man.

He did not even look at me. He was hopping around and crying out wildly to the boy.

"Dad, what's the matter?" the boy shouted again. He had hold of the man and was struggling to keep him on the top of the water.

Moving as fast as I could, I pulled off my shoes and dived in to the lake. I swam out and grabbed the man just as his weight was beginning to drag the boy down. With the boy's help, I towed him to shore.

I pulled out his mouth piece and turned to the boy. "What happened?"

The boy was breathing hard. "He—dived down—he went—just to look around. It—it was his first time down and—"

I looked at the man. It was easy to see that he was in great pain.

I ran to the jeep and got my air tanks and other diving gear.

"What is it?" cried the boy.

"He probably has an attack of the bends," I said as I strapped on my gear. "I haven't time to explain it now, but the point is he may have bubbles in his blood, and if I don't move fast, they may cripple him."

As a rule, a man suffering from the bends would be rushed to a special device called a decompression chamber. There, the bubbles in the blood can be reduced and dissolved before any lasting damage is done. But we were a good five hundred miles away from the nearest chamber. By the time we could reach it, it would be too late.

There was only one hope. I had to take this diver back in to the lake, and then I had to bring him up to the top by slow stages. That was the only way to rid his blood of those dangerous bubbles. Even so, I had to hope that his condition was not serious—or I could not be of help to him no matter what I did.

I said to the boy, "I'm taking him down. I know you don't understand, but you'll have to trust me."

I dragged the boy's father in to the water. Just before putting in my own mouth piece, I said, "We have to be down for a long time. When we come up, we will need blankets—hot soup—"

"All right," the boy said, "we will have everything ready."

"Make him well again!" shouted the old man. "That's all we ask."

We went down in to the lake, the stranger and I. It was cold and dark. I guided him down through the water, to a rock shelf where I could hold on. Once he was breathing compressed air deep in the water, the man would be in less pain. His expression showed that he did not understand why he was here. I tried to explain to him with hand signals, but he did not understand the skin-diving code. "He must be completely new to diving," I thought.

It was lucky that I had clipped my writing slate to my weight belt. I wrote on it: "Breathe deep and slow." He did as I asked, and I wrote: "When we go up, breathe in a normal way. Don't hold your breath."

He nodded.

Much later we started up, with me holding him by the wrist and guiding him. At regular stages, we stopped to tread water. I made sure that he was breathing properly. That was very important, for it was the only way he could rid himself of the gases that had caused the bends.

It was a long, slow climb up. The water was so cold that even I found myself wanting to speed things along and get to the surface faster. We were both trembling and shivering, but I forced myself to go slowly.

I checked the air in my tanks. Not much left. It was time to start up through the top layer of water. It was much brighter up here where the rays of the sun streamed down through the water. I brought the man up steadily, gesturing for him to go slowly.

Finally we broke water. He was so exhausted that he could not pull the mouth piece from his mouth. I was very tired, too. It took every bit of my strength to help him to the shore.

There was not much sun left, and a cold wind was blowing. I felt strong arms take hold of me and lift me out of the water.

"Here, take a swallow of this," the old man said. A cup of hot soup was thrust into my hands. I took a big swallow. Nothing in all my life had ever tasted so good.

I bent down and took a close look at the man I had rescued. His eyes were closed, but he was breathing steadily. I listened to his heart beat and said, "He's all right."

"Yahooo!" The old man took off his hat and flung it down and leaped in the air with joy. Then he did a wild little dance, slapping his leg and yelling, "I knew it, I knew he'd be all right! You can't kill a Clark. We are as tough as prairie dogs, and twice as smart!"

"Dad, Dad," the boy said happily as he hugged his father.

"Stranger, who are you?" the old man asked.

I shook my head and muttered, "Can't talk—"

I took another swallow of soup and stretched out near the fire.

"By gum, you really did it," continued the old man.

I closed my eyes as I heard him say, "You saved his life, you did. Whoever you are, I want you to know how grateful we are."

He was saying something else. But I was so exhausted that I drifted off into a deep sleep without hearing another word.

Chapter 2

HILLS OF GOLD

It was dawn when I woke. The sun was in my eyes, and there was a smell of coffee in the air. I looked up to see the old man staring down at me with a great big smile on his face.

"Rise and shine," he said. "It's a great day out. Smells as sweet and clean as a baby's breath. Have some coffee."

I sat up and rubbed the sleep from my eyes. The old man turned away and shouted, "Hey, Jim—Hardy! Come on over!" Then he turned back to me. "Now you can tell me your name. Mine is Gramps. They called me that even before I had a grandson. I guess I've always looked like an old man. Had a beard when I was 25, and it turned gray when I was 30. I'm 78 years old, but fit as a deer."

"And you make good coffee," I said with a laugh.

"Heck," he answered, "I've been cooking for myself for longer than I care to remember."

"My name is Bill," I told him. "Bill Bryan."

"Good morning," came another voice. It was the man I had saved yesterday.

"This is my son Hardy," said Gramps.

Hardy was a man in his late forties. He was not big but he had a sturdy build and a strong, open face that I liked on first sight.

"How do you feel?" I asked him.

"I feel good—thanks to you."

"Was yestrday the first time you ever dived?"

He nodded. "I sure made a mess of it, didn't I?"

Just then the boy came up. In one hand he held a long fishing pole, in the other, half a dozen lake trout.

"Lookee here," Gramps cried out. "Nice going, Jim!"

Now I had a chance to get a close look at the boy. He was taller than his father, but had the same sturdy build. I took a guess that the boy was 16 years old. He had black hair and a straight back, and he moved in an easy way. All three—grandfather, father and son—looked brown and strong.

"Jim, meet Bill Bryan," Hardy said.

Jim said hello and asked, "Are you a real diver, Mr. Bryan?"

"That's right. And call me Bill," I added. I turned to Hardy. "If yesterday was the first time, why did you take such a big risk?"

"I didn't think it would be so dangerous."

"Diving has to be learned, like anything else."

Hardy smiled a little. "What about the first skin divers? Didn't they have to learn by themselves? There wasn't anybody to teach them."

"The first men to skin dive didn't wear masks or heavy lead belts, or go down with air tanks on their shoulders. They dived just the way any swimmer would, by holding their breath," I answered.

"Men have been diving in to the sea for thousands of years, ever since the time of the ancient Greeks. They learned a lot about water pressure, what the dangers were of staying down and coming up too suddenly. Today's skin divers are only improving on all the things that have gone before."

Hardy told me, "I don't want to argue with you, but I've learned in life that experience is usually the best teacher."

"If you live to know what you've learned," I replied. "Yesterday, you almost didn't live. That's learning the hard way, seems to me."

"Exactly what did I do wrong?" Hardy asked. He wasn't arguing any more, he just wanted to know.

"You went wrong from the very minute you stepped in to the lake."

"I only wanted to test my new skin-diving gear. I had bought it just the day before."

"You should never dive alone," I said. "That is the first

rule of diving. The second is: understand what diving is all about."

"Tell you what," Gramps interrupted. "While you tell Hardy what he should know about skin diving, I will cook up this mess of fish that Jim has caught. Nothing like fresh trout for breakfast."

He took the fish and moved down to the edge of the lake. "Just keep talking," he said over his shoulder. "I can listen to you while I clean these fish."

Jim sat down next to his father. I smiled at father and son and said, "It would be impossible for me to explain the whole theory of diving to you over breakfast. But I will try to explain what causes a man to get the bends."

I put my thumb over the mouth of a bottle of soda I had in the jeep and shook it up. "See the bubbles? That's what happens to your body when you are diving deep. The gas bubbles go in to your cells and tissues. This is perfectly normal, and if you breathe properly, you won't have any trouble. As you come up to the surface—swimming slowly and breathing in and out—your body will pass off the gases like this."

I lifted my thumb gently from the mouth of the bottle. The gas hissed out slowly and quietly.

"But if you shoot right up, this will happen instead." Now I pressed my thumb down tightly and shook the bottle hard. I lifted my thumb. The soda shot up in a stream that showered all over us.

"Of course, that is not a complete explanation—but it

19

gives you the picture. The reason why I took you back down in to the lake," I went on, "was to get you back to the same water pressure you had been under before. You know, don't you, that water has weight?"

They nodded.

"The deeper you go, the heavier the weight of water is," I went on. "When this weight presses on your lungs, gas bubbles form, just the way they did when I shook the bottle. If a skin diver goes up to the surface too fast, there's no time for the blood stream to pass off the gas. If the diver goes up in easy stages, the pressure gradually becomes less, and the body has time to get rid of the bubbles. There are lists, called decompression tables, which tell a diver at what rate it is safe for him to come up out of the water. It all depends on how deep you went and how long you stayed. You were lucky, Hardy."

He nodded. "You were right, Bill," he said. "There is a lot to know about diving."

"If you plan to do much diving, you had better find yourself a good teacher."

"I told him that," said Gramps. "But he wouldn't listen. He's a Clark, you see. The Clarks have always made up their own minds."

"How long have you lived in these hills?" I asked.

"My daddy took part in the first great gold rush," Gramps said. He was frying the fish now, and the smell of them reminded me that I was very hungry.

"He came here from San Antonio," Gramps continued. "The cry had gone up that gold could be had in these hills. The men came flooding in. Some were tough, hard-riding, hard-living men like my daddy. They weren't men, they were *giants!* They worked fourteen, sixteen hours a day. They lived on dried bread and water, and slept under the stars.

"Others were not so tough. They did not know what they were letting themselves in for. They thought the gold would be hanging from the trees like peaches. Lots of them starved to death—or froze to death up in these hills. Gets powerful cold up here at night, even in summer. Others caught sick and limped back to wherever

they had come from. A few made their pile, though. Yes, sir, even some city folk stumbled on to gold.

"Of course," Gramps went on, "there was lots more gold in those days than there is now. Some men made millions before the boom gave out."

"How did your father make out?" I asked.

"My daddy?" Gramps grinned widely. "He made a couple of fortunes—and blew them just like that. What a man!" Gramps finished proudly.

He was passing out portions of the cooked fish. It tasted as good as it smelled. I ate quickly, sopping up the juices with big hunks of bread that Gramps had made earlier this morning.

"What happened to your father finally?" I asked, between bites.

"He died right up here in these hills," Gramps told me. "The gold rush was over by then. Most of the miners had gone, leaving behind an awful mess—flooded mines, caved-in mines, heaps of gravel and rocks."

"The Clarks have been in these hills for over a hundred years," Hardy chimed in, "and we expect to be here for another hundred."

"What about your wife?" I asked Hardy.

"She loved these hills as much as I did," Hardy told me. "She died a few years after Jim was born."

Gramps sighed. "The Clarks have never had good luck."

"Lots of folks are worse off than we," said Hardy.

"After all, we have this camp here and all this land."

I looked around at the lake and hills. "How much of this is yours?"

Now Jim spoke up for the first time. "All of it," he said proudly. "The lake and all the land from here to there." He pointed to a hill that stood a good half mile away.

"I bought this land fifteen years ago from some local people," Gramps said. "In the old days these hills contained two of the richest mines of all. One was buried by a land slide which no man will ever be able to clear. The other was flooded."

"There is the entrance to it over there," said Jim, pointing off to the left. I looked and saw nothing but water. "The mouth of the mine sits just a few feet under the surface of the lake. You can see it from a rowboat."

"That's why we bought all this skin-diving gear," Hardy explained. "We thought there must be gold down in the mine—and we mean to bring it up."

"There is lots of it down there!" Gramps put in. "My daddy used to talk about that mine. He said it would take a hundred years to pick it clean."

"Then how come you were able to buy it?" I asked.

"When I bought it, there was no such thing as skin diving. A flooded mine was considered of no worth. Do you know how much I paid for it?" Gramps asked. "I paid a thousand dollars for the whole property. Then I said, *How much do you want for the flooded mine?* They threw it in for an extra hundred dollars. A hundred dollars!" he repeated and burst into joyful laughter. "That's all I paid for it—and it may be worth a hundred times that today!"

"Don't be so sure," Hardy said. "We might get down there and discover that your daddy didn't know what he was talking about."

"We will see," Gramps said. "First you and Jim learn how to use all this diving gear. Then we will find out what kind of mine we have."

Hardy studied me closely, not saying anything for a moment. Then he said slowly, "Bill, I would like to ask you something. Would you be interested in working this mine with us? It is plain from what happened yesterday that we need a good diving teacher. If you take the job, we will cut you in as a partner. You can keep one-third of whatever we bring up out of there."

"It would be a good deal all around," Gramps said. "We need you and you need us."

"How do you figure that?" I asked.

"Well, if you start searching for gold on your own, it will take you a long time to learn the ropes. And you might not find any. But if you come in with us, you will be getting quick action. We can teach you a few things, too, you know. We may not know how to dive, but we are good miners. If there's any gold down there, we will bring it up. Besides," he added with a smile, "you won't find a better cook than me within two hundred miles."

I laughed. "That's for sure, Gramps. But I'm afraid I must turn you down."

"Why?" Jim wanted to know.

"Maybe after I learn my way around a little better, I will come back and join you," I answered. "Right now I think I'd better stay on my own."

Disappointment showed on their faces—particularly Jim's. "All right," Hardy said. "But be careful. There has been a lot of trouble around here lately. New divers aren't exactly welcome in some parts." I thought of the letter from Arnie Lewis. He had warned me, too.

"Thanks," I said. "Now I'd better be going."

I gathered up my things and dumped them in to the jeep. Then I remembered that I wanted to give Hardy something. It was a book.

"Here," I said, handing it to him. "This is a book for beginners about diving. It tells some of the first things you should know. It's better if you work with someone who has experience, but the book will help some. And don't be in such a hurry. Go slow. Take it easy as you learn."

Hardy took the book. "Thanks, Bill," he said. "I'm not much of a reader but I will certainly study this book."

"You read it too, Jim," I added, turning to the boy.

Hardy handed the book to his son. Jim looked through the pages and gave a mighty sigh. "If only it didn't have so many big words," he said finally.

I laughed and climbed in to the jeep. "Good-by," I called to them.

"Good-by," Jim said. He stuck his hand out and we

shook firmly. "Be careful." I was sorry to be leaving the Clarks. I liked the kind of people they were.

"Good-by, good-by," they were shouting. "Come back and see us soon."

"I will!" I answered as I pointed the jeep up the side of the hill. Soon I was on the road once more. As I shifted into high, I glanced down at the camp and saw the Clarks still standing by the fire, waving to me.

Chapter 3

TROUBLE IN THE STREETS

I reached Hilltown about an hour later. It looked like the main street in a cowboy movie—general store, hotel, a few shops and houses. The streets were dusty. There were wooden sidewalks. I had the feeling that a strong wind would blow everything away.

Groups of men stood around wearing cowboy pants, shirts and hats, guns strapped to their hips. Every eye was on me—the new man in town. The faces wore no particular expression. I passed a man riding along on a pony. He was the sheriff, and he had a badge and a big mustache.

"Gramps' daddy would feel right at home here," I thought. "It's hard to believe that a place like this can still exist in the twentieth century."

Spotting a sign reading "Hotel," I pulled to a halt in

front of the old building and went inside. The main room was furnished with pieces that looked left over from the days of '49. A noisy fan turned slowly over my head, scarcely stirring the hot air.

There was a bell on the desk with a sign saying "Please Ring." When I did, a man came out of the back room. He was big and fat. His face was sweating, and he kept wiping it with a damp, dirty handkerchief.

"I'm looking for a room," I said.

"Full up," he told me shortly.

"I have a sleeping bag. I can sleep anywhere—on the floor, in this room—"

"No room anywhere. Every inch of space is taken. This town is loaded with miners, Mister. When night comes you can't walk through the main room here for the sleeping bodies."

"Is there another hotel in town?"

"Nope. You'd better sleep up in the hills. Make your own camp."

"I'd prefer to sleep in town my first night here."

"Well, I can't help you," he said.

"Can I get a room in a private house?"

He mopped his face, examining me some more. No wonder Arnie Lewis had complained of the strange ways of these people. I practically had to squeeze an answer out of him.

"Try down at the general store. The Maxwells own a lot of property around here. Maybe they can put you up."

I went out in to the bright sunlight again, tasting the dust of the town, and drove to the general store. Goods of all kinds were piled up in its windows—everything from food to camping equipment. There was one window full of the latest skin-diving gear. But the prices they were asking! Simple things like face masks cost four times what they were worth anywhere else!

The same held true for the cost of food. Oranges went for half a dollar each, a quart of milk for twice that much. As I stood there blinking at the prices, I felt someone else's eyes on me. I looked up and saw a man about my own age. He had a mean face that had not been shaved. He did not say a word, just stood there looking from me to the jeep and back. I stared back at him, not liking the way he was sizing me up. Finally, I walked past him and entered the store.

A man was standing behind the counter, putting cans on the shelf. He was small and had a nervous face—eyes that blinked too much, a trembling mouth.

"Yes?"

"I'm looking for a place to sleep."

"This is a general store, not a hotel," said a voice from behind me. It was the man who had been staring at me outside.

"The man in the hotel sent me down to see you."

The face showed no expression.

"That is a heap of good equipment you have in that jeep outside. Especially that air compressor."

"I see you have one yourself," I said, indicating the machine standing in a corner of the store.

"That's right," he said. "And we are in the market for another one."

"I'm not interested in selling."

The one behind the counter said, "We will give you two hundred and fifty."

"I said no."

"Three hundred," the other put in.

"It's not for sale," I said firmly. "Besides, I don't know what your names are."

"I'm Nance Maxwell," said the one with the mean look. "And this is my brother, Bert. We—"

"Look," I interrupted. "All I want is a place to sleep for a few nights."

"And all we want is your compressor. We will pay good money for it. You can take it in cash or gold chunks."

"It's not for sale," I repeated.

"No sale, no room," said Nance.

Our eyes met, and then I turned away and walked out. After starting up the jeep and turning a corner, I suddenly realized that I did not know where I wanted to go. I found myself on a side street behind a row of stores. One sign read "Coffee Shop," so I pulled in to a side alley and parked the jeep.

I would sit over a cup of coffee for a while and think out my next move.

The man behind the counter was a big Indian

with black hair. "You the new man for skin diving?" he asked after taking my order.

"How did you know?"

"Word travels fast in this town."

"They don't like new people very much, do they?"

"Everybody has gold on his mind," the Indian said. "Gold does funny things to men."

"Do you know the Maxwells?" I asked him.

"I know everybody here."

I drank my coffee. "They just offered to buy my compressor. Offered me three times what it's worth."

The Indian nodded. "They know what they are doing," he said. "They own the only other air compressor within 300 miles of Hilltown. Anybody who wants to fill up his air tanks has to pay whatever they ask."

So that was it. The Maxwells thought that I meant to threaten their business. They were probably afraid I was going to charge less than they. But if they bought my compressor, everyone would still have to come to them, and they could charge what they pleased.

"It's the gold," the Indian went on. "I've known the Maxwells a long time, but it's only recently that they have become so greedy. They used to be nice fellows."

"But they own a store and property. They seem to be doing well."

"It's not enough. Nothing is ever enough in a gold rush. Unless a man owns a working mine, he will never be satisfied. That's what gold fever is."

"And you?" I asked. "Don't you have gold fever?"

"No," he said. "I'm not like these people. I'm not like you either. I am an Indian. My people were here before the white man came. This was our country. We lived here and never worried about gold. The fish, the deer—these were important things to us.

"Then the white man came and killed my people or shoved them off the land. I'm waiting for the day when the gold runs out, and the white man leaves for good. Then I will go back up in to the hills, with my wife and children. The hills will belong to their original owners again."

He spoke quietly, without anger or hate. When he finished, he stood looking down at me, a giant of a man, as big and strong as the hills he talked about.

I paid my bill, went out and walked toward the jeep. The town was quiet now, and the streets were deserted. People were probably avoiding the strong heat of noon by staying inside.

When I turned into the alley where the jeep was parked, I saw something that brought me up short. There was Bert Maxwell, climbing in to the car!

He shot a surprised, frightened look at me and slid behind the wheel. I broke in to a run. I had left the key in the switch.

He was starting the motor when I reached him. I grabbed his arm and dragged him from under the wheel.

"Let me go," he shouted. At the same time he swung

his fist at me. But I was ready, and the blow glanced off my shoulder. Then he wrapped his arms around my legs and tumbled me to the ground. As we rolled in the dust, he tried to get his hands around my throat. But I broke his hold, all the while seeing the terrible fear in his eyes. I pulled him to his feet and shoved him up against a wall.

"Don't hit me," he whined.

"Why were you trying to steal my jeep?"

"I was not—"

I held him tight and gave him a hard slap across the face. He shook his head furiously, crying, "I made a mistake—"

He glanced at something behind me. I turned—but too late. A tremendous blow caught me on the back of the neck, sending me to my knees. Almost knocked out, it was all I could do to roll out of the way.

Through misted eyes I could make out Nance Maxwell's face. I scrambled to my feet, swinging my fists. By then Bert Maxwell was back in the fight, attacking from behind.

As I drew my arm back again, I was pinned from behind by powerful arms.

"That's enough," a voice barked in my ear.

Nance, down on all fours, stared up at me. Bert Maxwell, pressing a handkerchief to his bleeding mouth, stepped forward. He pointed at me and said, "That's him, Sheriff, the one who started the fight—"

"That's a lie," I said.

33

"Hold on now," the sheriff put in. "Let Bert talk."

Bert continued. "I was walking home, passing through the alley, when this fellow jumped me."

"He started the fight!" I protested. "He was trying to steal my jeep—"

"I said, let him talk!"

Bert said, "He came in to the store earlier. Said he was broke, wanted me to give him some goods on credit. I refused him, and he got mad. I had to order him out of the store."

The sheriff turned to Nance. "Were you in the store then?"

"I was," he said. "Bert is telling the truth, Sheriff."

"He must have waited here in the alley for me," said Bert. "Soon as I passed, he grabbed me from behind."

Now the sheriff looked at me. "What have you got to say?"

"It's all a lie. I didn't have any trouble with them in the store. They are after my compressor. I caught Bert trying to steal it."

The sheriff frowned. "There's nothing I can do but take you in. You are a stranger. These men are respected citizens. I will have to let the judge decide."

He told me to get in the jeep. I did, and he sat beside me, hand on his gun. "Meet us at the court house," he told the Maxwells.

We drove to the court house, a low little brick building a block away. The sheriff led me to his office, where he booked me and took my finger prints. After collecting my possessions and locking them up, he led me through the rear of the building to a jail cell.

"This is all wrong," I said. "I haven't done anything."

"You may be right," he answered, "but my job is to keep law and order. You can tell your story to the judge. Lucky for you he's holding court tomorrow."

"What about my jeep?"

"It will be safe outside." The sheriff took a ring of keys from his pocket. "We've had nothing but trouble with you skin-diving fellows the last few months," he said. "I wish all of you would stop coming here. There are too many gold miners around already."

He opened the cell door. "See you in the morning," he said. Then he locked the door and walked away.

The cell was a small one. There was an iron cot, a wash stand and one tiny barred window. The air in the cell smelled stale and dirty.

My heart sank. I felt more miserable than I had ever felt in my life. I could hear Arnie Lewis's words echoing in my head: "Watch your step when you arrive . . . watch yourself at all times . . . there are sharks everywhere. . . ."

My head had begun to ache. I lay back on the hard, smelly mattress and stared up at the bars on the window.

Chapter 4

A BAD CASE OF GOLD FEVER

I did not sleep much that night. Mostly I lay awake trying to figure out why the Maxwells had attacked me and why they had lied to the sheriff. Finally, when it was almost dawn, I fell in to a light sleep. The next thing I knew, I was being shaken awake.

"Wake up, Mister. Time to go to court."

Breakfast was a few pieces of stale bread and a mug of weak coffee. When I had swallowed it, the sheriff unlocked my cell and said, "This way, Mister."

I followed him down a long hall to the court room. It was a small room, plainly furnished with a few benches and chairs, with a high stand in front, on which the judge sat.

A lot of the people from the town were there when I

entered. I recognized many of their faces. These were the men who had stared at me when I arrived the day before. Now they regarded me with dislike. I was not only a stranger, but a trouble maker.

Of all the faces, only one seemed friendly, and that was the Indian's. He sat in the first row of the crowd, staring quietly at me. He was the biggest man in the room, towering head and shoulders above everyone else.

The judge entered. He was tall and thin and wore a fancy white shirt with a black string tie. He got some small matters out of the way—property fights and such—and then called my case. More people crowded into the room, including Bert and Nance Maxwell. They both were wearing clean clothes, and looked smart and important. I realized that I was still wearing the clothes I had fought in. They were ripped and dirty. Blood stains showed on my shirt.

I had no chance at the trial. It was my word against the Maxwells', and they were big men in these parts. The judge could do nothing but accept their story as truth. Anyway, they were two to my one.

Not even the Indian could help me. I told the court that I had been drinking coffee in his shop at the time Bert Maxwell claimed I was picking a fight with him, and the Indian came forward and backed me up as best he could. But he was not sure of the exact time I had entered the shop, nor could he say how much time I had spent there. Everything was against me.

Soon the judge was saying, "I find you guilty, but since you are new here, and there is some element of doubt about the case, I will not sentence you to jail. I'm going to set a fine. If you can pay it, you will be free to leave. I suggest you head for another town, but that's up to you. At any rate, the fine is $200."

"$200?" I did not have anything like that much!

"$200 or thirty days in jail," said the judge.

Thirty days in that gray little cell? The thought made me sick. So, for the first time in my life, I found myself pleading for mercy: "Judge, I ask you to change that sentence. Even if I were guilty, it would be only a first offense. Isn't that a pretty steep fine for a first offense?"

"Sorry, Mr. Bryan," said the judge.

"Well, then, how about letting me work it off? Perhaps I will find some gold. If I do, I will give the court a share of it. . . ."

"Do you think everybody who comes to Hilltown finds gold? If that were the case, we would all be rich men." The judge called out, "Sheriff, return this man to his cell."

Suddenly Nance Maxwell spoke: "Hold on, Judge." Everyone turned to look. "I have an idea that might make everyone happy," Nance said. "Me and my brother don't really want to send this fellow to jail, even if he did pick a fight with us. Seeing how he can't pay his fine, why don't we let him pay it off in goods instead of money?"

"What kind of goods?" the judge asked.

"Well, he arrived in town with an air compressor.

That's worth pretty good money. In fact, we will buy it from him for the cost of the fine."

So *that* was it! That was why the Maxwells had picked a fight with me. They had not really been trying to steal the compressor—all they had wanted was to find a way to get their hands on it in a legal way! Once that happened, they would still own the only air compressors in these parts. And skin divers would still have to pay through the nose to get air for their tanks!

"Hold it! I will pay his fine." This voice came from the back of the court room. I looked up and saw Hardy Clark.

An excited murmur swept through the court. Hardy pushed his way forward.

"Do you know this man?" asked the judge.

"I do," said Hardy. "And I have enough gold dust on me to set him free."

The judge looked at me. "You want it this way?"

"If it's all right with Mr. Clark."

The judge said to the sheriff, "Let him go."

A few moments later I was standing outside the court house with Hardy Clark. "It's a good thing I decided to come to town this morning," Hardy said.

I grinned. "It sure is! Now my only problem is how to pay you back."

"Well, my offer of a job still goes. Anyway, we Clarks owe you a great deal. You saved my life. And, Bill, we need you badly out there."

We were walking toward the jeep.

"But don't get me wrong," Hardy added. "I don't want you to take this job because you feel you owe it to me. I will trust you for the money, no matter what."

That did it. I climbed behind the wheel of the jeep and said, "Where's your car? You lead the way out to the camp. I will be right behind you."

Hardy's face cracked in to a big smile.

Hardy and I reached the camp about lunch time. Gramps was bending over a fire, and even from a distance the breeze brought me the good smell of the stew he was cooking. The smell made me remember that I had had nothing to eat since yesterday except stale bread.

"Well, lookee here!" cried Gramps when he spied me. "Where did you fall from, Bill boy?"

"He's come to join us," Hardy answered.

Gramps pulled off his hat and flung it high in the air. "Yipppeee!" Then, turning, he cupped his hands and called up into the hills, "Hey, Jim, come and see who's here!"

Soon Jim came into sight. He was riding a mule and holding a rifle in one arm. Coming up to us, he got quickly off his mule and came over to shake hands. There was a big smile on his face. "Hi, Bill! Golly, I'm glad to see you."

"I'm glad to be here," I told him—and I certainly was!

A few minutes later we all sat down to lunch around the fire. I told Gramps and Jim what had happened.

"The Indian said the Maxwells are mad because they don't own any working mines. He said they are suffering from a bad case of gold fever," Hardy Clark added.

"It's a funny thing," said Gramps, "but the last big mine they owned was this one right here."

That made me sit up. "You mean you bought the flooded mine from them?"

"From their daddy, actually. We sometimes worked together in the old days. He sold this site to me when he took sick in his old age. Knew he was about to die, I guess. Anyway, with the money he left them, the boys went out and bought a lot of town property. They decided to become merchants instead of miners. Now I suppose they regret it."

"No use thinking about that now," I said. "It's over and done with. So let's get to the business at hand."

As we ate, we discussed the best way to begin work on the mine. The Clarks were eager to dive down into its flooded depths to see whether there was any gold down there. "Who knows, maybe all we will find is a lot of gravel and rocks," Hardy said.

"I think I should go down first for a careful look around," I said.

"I thought you said that a person should never go down alone," said Jim.

"That's right, but in this case I have no choice. I can't permit you or Hardy to dive until you are properly trained. Remember, the under-water world is entirely different from dry land. It has its own laws and rules. You must learn to accept those rules.

"I know you are eager to have a look at the mine," I continued, "but it will have to wait until you have learned more about diving—enough so that you can go down and be certain of coming up again. Diving for gold is work, not play. And it's hard work."

I did not do any diving that day. I wanted to get my things out of the jeep and inspect my equipment. Jim and Hardy helped me put up my tent. It took most of the afternoon to get things arranged. I finished the day with a swim, and then it was meal time again. Gramps entertained us after dinner with some of his tales. He knew hundreds of them, mostly funny stories about the Old West. He kept us laughing while he remembered some of the crazy names the miners of '49 gave to their towns.

"These towns used to spring up over night. Somebody would come along and slap a few boards together, smear the roof over with mud, and call it home. The names were a way of making fun of those places—the miners were kidding themselves. Why, my daddy lived for three months in a place he called Hen Roost Camp. There were some others, like Seven-by-Nine Valley and Mud Springs and Pancake Hill. But my favorite was a place called Hog's Rest."

Here Gramps slapped his leg and laughed his big laugh. "Can you imagine writing home and telling your folks you were living in a place called Hog's Rest? You can bet that nobody dared write 'Wish you were here' in a letter like that!"

I was still laughing when I turned in that night. The sleeping bag felt good under me, and the night air was clean and cold. I fell asleep in a matter of minutes.

In the morning I ate lightly—it is not a good idea to have too much in your stomach when you dive—and suited up. I put on my thickest wet suit—a kind of diving suit. This one had a heavy lining of nylon.

It was good to be diving again. The feel of the water, as I went down into it, was different from the way the sea feels. It was heavier and far colder. Also, it was darker, and there was a powerful current. I fought it as I dived toward the spot where the entrance to the mine was supposed to be. It took me some time to locate it.

Things looked strange down here. There were few fish

and little of the plant life that grows in the sea. Instead, odd bits and pieces of equipment from the old mine showed among dark weeds and big rocks. Finally, I located the mouth of the mine. I swam toward it, fighting the current, which was fed by mountain streams emptying into the lake.

Now I entered the mine. The shaft was narrow and dark. I used an old Navy flash light to light the way. The shaft led straight down, then leveled off and opened up wide, like a fan. Many other shafts ran out from it. I swam on down to the bottom.

I had intended to spend some time looking for nuggets of gold, but it was too much of a struggle in the current.

I did get a quick look around, though. I saw many things from the old days, when men like Gramps crawled down here and hacked out these shafts with pick and shovel. I could still see wheelbarrows which had been left there when the mine was flooded.

The current was causing me to use up more air than usual, because of all the energy it took to fight it. There was nothing to do but begin the slow rise to the surface. I had only been down about a half hour, but already I was cold.

When I broke water, Gramps was waiting to ask, "Well? What did you see?"

"Any gold?" Jim put in eagerly.

They were looking at me with such hopeful faces that I hated to answer them. "I didn't find anything. Conditions are very difficult. It's very cold, and the current is impossible."

"Does that mean that the mine can not be worked?"

"I don't know. The first thing we must do is block off some of the mountain streams that pour into the mine."

I began changing into dry clothes. "I'm not sure," I said, "but maybe we can do it with special under-water dynamite."

"Won't that blow the mine to bits?"

"No, not if it's placed right. We need to throw up a heap of stones and gravel to form a dam."

"Do you know anything about under-water dynamite?" asked Hardy.

"I was a frog man in the Navy. We often worked with it. The question is, is it available in these parts? Have you seen any for sale in Hilltown?"

Hardy shook his head. "No, but there might be some in Sonora."

"Where is that?"

"About a hundred miles from here."

"Well, we should go there and have a look."

"If we do manage to dam up the streams, will we be able to work the mine for sure?" Jim asked.

"I don't know," was my answer. "It's very dangerous down there."

They stood silent now, worry showing on their faces. Then Gramps spat on his leathery palms and rubbed them together. "Well, what are we so gloomy about? There's still a chance, isn't there? So, what if the work is dangerous? Since when have the Clarks been afraid of danger?"

The four of us stood staring down silently into the dark lake. This was the real agony of a miner's life, knowing that all your work, all your hopes and dreams, might come to nothing in the end. We were going to risk our lives down in that mine and there was no guarantee that we would find even so much as an ounce of gold for our trouble.

Chapter 5

THE GREAT DISCOVERY

The next day, Hardy drove to Sonora and came back with the dynamite we needed. "Good," I said. "Now we can really set to work."

I spent the mornings setting the charges. In the afternoons, I started teaching Jim and Hardy the basics of diving. First, I explained the equipment—mask, fins, air tank, mouth piece, wet suit.

"You see this thing that looks like a watch?" I said. "Well, that's a depth gauge—it tells you how deep you are in the water. You keep your eye on that, Hardy—we don't want any more cases of the bends."

Hardy and Jim both nodded gravely.

I worked on their swimming style a little. Jim was fine, but Hardy needed to practice the various kicks a skin diver needs. We also practiced surface dives and the art of balancing ear pressure.

Next I showed them how to check their equipment, how to look for air leaks, and how to breathe properly. I showed them the hand signals that divers use, and we practiced them over and over. Finally, I took them to the shallow part of the lake for their first dive.

Hardy followed me down slowly and cautiously, doing everything right. I signaled to him, "Fine . . . okay. . . ."

We swam along ten feet below the surface. Everything was working perfectly. But this was too tame for Jim. He swam farther and farther ahead, and when he spotted a rusty old wheel below us, he dived down to look at it.

He was so interested that he did not see my signal. I had to bang on my air tank with my knife to get his attention. But when he saw me jabbing my thumb toward the surface, he swam obediently back, and we returned to the surface.

I removed my mouth piece and lifted my mask. "Now, what did I tell you about sticking close to me?"

"There wasn't any danger," Jim protested. "You explore alone, don't you?"

"This is your first dive. When you have a little more experience behind you, then you can go off on your own."

Jim agreed, and for the rest of the afternoon he did everything exactly as I had taught him.

But he worried me. He learned more by copying me than by understanding why. This helped him to learn fast—and he *was* good, no denying that. But it made me wonder if he could be trusted in case of trouble. With this in mind, I took him down and drilled him hard in taking off and putting on his diving gear under water.

First I made him sit on the bottom and remove his weight belt. Once it was draped across his legs, he could then undo the straps of his harness, slip off his air tanks, and turn off the air on the tanks. Then the trick was to take a half breath, remove the mouth piece and start swimming up, breathing out steadily as he rose.

In order to put on the gear, he had to descend and take hold of the tanks that were weighted down like an anchor. Then he had to pick up the mouth piece, with the air flowing out of it, and place it in his mouth—clearing the hose with a sharp blast of breath.

Jim finally learned this drill pretty well. I taught it to Hardy, too, but he was less sure of himself. He could not get used to the feeling of being so far down in the water without air to breathe. He would have to learn what he did not know while on the job.

Now that I had Jim and Hardy to help me, I managed to string the entire line of dynamite in two more days. The actual stringing itself was not too difficult. The hard thing was deciding where to place the charges. One charge in the wrong place might send tons of stone tumbling down into the entrance of the under-water mine. I made a dozen exploring trips to be sure that they were right.

8S130

Finally we were ready. I set the last charge and surfaced. With the Clarks watching, I set off the charge, and we ducked.

There was a deep *boom!* Then a huge column of water shot up, carrying with it rocks and dirt and stones. They plunged back into the water with great splashes, sending waves high up on the shore. But when the water settled and the air cleared, we could see that a rough wall of earth had been thrown up.

"It looks good," said Gramps.

"We won't know for sure whether the streams are blocked off, until we dive down and take a look," I said. "Meanwhile, we should make that rough wall nice and water tight."

We set to work with shovels, packing the wall down and filling in the empty spots. It was hard work under the hot sun. By the middle of the morning the heat was like a blast furnace, burning into my skin and eyes. I found myself wondering what I was doing here in this crazy country, where it was fiercely hot by day and sharply cold by night. What I would have given then for a sight of my lovely ocean!

Living like this made me admire the Clarks all the more, especially Gramps. He did his share of hard labor without complaining. And when he wasn't working, he was either cooking something good to eat or singing a song or telling a funny tale. He was never still, never silent. His bright eyes flashed and twinkled. When I looked at him—in his seventies and still going strong—I thought twice about complaining.

Nobody, not even the Clarks, could work long out in the noon-day sun. That was the time to find some shade and either sleep or read. It was too hot to read in my tent, so I would walk up into the hills and sit in the shade of some tall pine trees. One day while I was taking it easy, I saw Jim approaching.

He was carrying his rifle and seemed surprised to see me there. "Something wrong, Jim?"

"No, no." He shook his head and without another word, turned and tramped away.

I did not think anything of this, but when I returned to camp later I could hear Jim saying to Hardy and Gramps: ". . . and do you know what he was doing?"

"No, what?" asked Gramps.

"Reading a book!" said Jim. "It's funny. Bill is such a regular guy, but there he was—reading a *book!*"

At that I could not contain myself. I burst into loud laughter and walked down to the camp. "Jim," I said, "I didn't mean to listen to your conversation, but I couldn't help it. Do you really think that there is something sissy about reading?"

Jim blushed, but he had the courage to answer honestly: "Yes, I do."

"Then you must think I'm a sissy?"

Jim was blushing furiously. "What I mean is that I *used* to think everybody who read was a sissy."

"But you don't think so any more?"

"Aw," Jim said, turning away, "I don't know what I think any more."

The next morning I dived down to the mine. The blasting had been successful. All the streams were blocked off beautifully. The water was still cold, but there was no current to fight. I returned to the top and reported to the Clarks that the job was perfect.

"Now we can start bringing up the gold," said Gramps.

"No, there are still other things we must do before that," I said. "First we must build a raft to hold all the machinery we will need on the job. And then I'd better dive down and see if there's any gold to be had."

"That's right," said Hardy. "No use knocking ourselves out until we know whether or not there's gold in that mine."

After a very light lunch, I suited up and got ready to go down. Jim helped me on with my harness.

"Bill," he said, "I'm sorry for what I said yesterday. It was stupid of me to talk like that."

"That's all right, Jim. If you hadn't lived in these hills all your life, you'd be used to books."

"I guess I have a lot to learn," he said.

I mussed his hair and said, "Don't worry about it, Jim. Learning never killed anybody."

Then I clipped my weight belt and waded out into the water, carrying my Navy flash light and a pick. I went down slowly, soon coming to the big part of the mine. I wondered which shaft to explore. Finally I picked a middle shaft, thinking it might lead to something good. Keeping close to the ground, I swam through it.

All of a sudden I had a funny feeling. When you dive a lot, you develop a sixth sense about danger. Usually it works in the presence of a shark, one of the most dangerous customers in the sea. But this time it was working for some other reason.

I looked around and saw that I had come face to face with a sharp drop in the floor of the mine. I shone my light down, but even this powerful beam did not reveal the bottom of the pit. Everything in me told me not to dive down in to it.

But I forced myself to go and take a look. I had to know where it led. Perhaps it was only a black hole which held no surprises. Then again, maybe it led to another level of the mine—maybe the level that contained the most gold. At any rate I had to go down, if only to be able to warn the others about it.

On the way down I flashed my light here and there. I saw many other shafts—some small, some large—leading every which way. I went down one of them. It crossed over into another shaft, and I turned down that one. Then, changing my mind, I turned back and tried to find the first shaft. No luck. For a short while, I lost my head. I gave in to fear—something a diver must never do. I went down one shaft after another—paths leading nowhere.

I stopped, took stock, made an effort to move slowly in a pattern instead of swimming around foolishly, wasting precious energy and air. Finally, after what seemed a long while, I worked my way back to where I had started.

Breathing a big sigh of relief, I swam up through the pit to the main part of the mine.

Choosing another passage, I set to work with my pick. I chopped away in a corner, trying to clear off some of the top layer of stones and gravel. Then I shone my light down the crack and looked for nuggets. Gramps had said they would shine yellow in the light.

The work was hard and slow. And it was lonely down in this dark shaft. A few fish swam by. They were not at all frightened, but they seemed surprised to see me. I began to find lumps that looked like metal ore, but I could not tell whether or not they were gold. In spite of what Gramps had said, they did not shine at all. He had not realized that everything down here would be coated with a thick layer of slime.

The only thing to do was gather up lumps and bring them to the surface. I had used up enough air anyway, and I was very cold.

When I broke water, I saw the Clarks waiting with hopeful looks on their faces. I pulled out my mouth piece and said, "Have a look at these." Gramps took the sack of ore and dumped it out at his feet. They each grabbed a lump and started scraping away at them eagerly with pen knives.

"This one is just a stone," Jim said quickly, tossing it aside.

"This one too," said Hardy. He picked up another and scraped the slime away.

Suddenly Gramps let out a howl. "Yahoo! Yahoo! Look at this!" he cried, waving a lump around wildly in the air. The ore showed bits of yellow.

"Gold!" he yelled. "A real nugget of gold!"

He took off his hat and sailed it high in the air. Then we were all shouting, joy and excitement bursting from us like water from a dam.

"Hallelujah!" cried Gramps. He was so happy that he could scarcely speak. He was dancing around like mad, face flushed, eyes sparkling like fireflies.

"I knew you'd do it!" cried Jim. He rushed up and threw his arms around me. "You did it, Bill!"

"Wait a minute," I told him. "I didn't put the gold

57

there. Nature did that. And I didn't find the mine. Gramps did that."

"It would have taken us months to learn how to dive," Hardy said. "You've brought us luck, Bill."

"Are you sure that we've hit it big?" I asked. "Maybe there's only a handful of nuggets there."

"No," said Gramps, "when you get a sample like this, you know you've hit a rich vein." He thrust the nugget under my nose and waved it around. "This baby is heavy with gold," he told me. "Can't you see it shining like the moon at midnight?"

Hardy and Gramps and Jim began to talk about how much the mine was worth and what they would do with all the money it would bring them. The government's fixed price for gold was $35 a fine ounce. But if the nuggets were sold in their raw form to museums or to people for their collections, a hunk like this would bring as much as $260. Immediately they began to multiply this figure by a hundred, a thousand. . . .

"Hold on," I said. "Don't count. . . ." But it was no use. Trying to curb their excitement was like trying to tell the ocean tide not to come in.

"First thing I'm going to buy is a new set of store teeth," said Gramps. "And I'm going to have them made out of gold. How's that, hah?" He laughed. "How would you like to see me with my mouth full of gold teeth? Why, when I smiled, I'd light up like a sign."

"I'm going to buy a new rifle," said Jim.

"Heck, you can buy five rifles!" Hardy told him.

I tried again. "Hey, wait a minute. Calm down!"

They all looked at me.

"I don't want to spoil your fun, but there are some things about the mine you should know."

They waited.

"First of all, the work will be slow and difficult. It's cold and dark down there, and a man can't stay down long. No matter how hard we work, we won't be able to bring up more than a few loads a day."

"A few loads like this every day, and we won't have a worry in the world," said Gramps.

"You are wrong," I said. "There's a lot to worry about down there. Today I found many shafts that cross back and forth over each other. If one of us got trapped in there, he might never get out. Even when we are not near that spot, we must never become careless, for it might cost us our lives."

That quieted them down.

"All right, Bill," said Hardy. "You don't have to say any more. We will try to be careful when we are diving."

"For your sake, I hope you will," I said. Then I turned to Gramps. "How about some food, you old goat?"

"Coming up." Gramps laughed. "Coming right up!"

Chapter 6

TROUBLE UNDER WATER

\

I had read about the gold fever that took hold of men in the great gold rush a hundred years ago. Now I was learning what gold fever really meant—knowing that there was a fortune just waiting for you to come and pick it up.

I got our under-water operation into action as fast as possible.

"First," I explained to Jim and to Hardy, "we build a raft. We can anchor it directly over the entrance to the old mine. Then, right on the raft, we put together the machinery that we need to dredge up the gold."

We made the raft by lashing together empty gasoline drums and putting a platform of boards over it. Then we had to get the dredging machinery together and make sure that the motor was running properly.

All the time we were assembling the machinery, Jim kept firing questions at me. One thing about that boy—you never had to explain anything twice.

"It's a shame Jim isn't getting some formal education," I remarked once to his father. "He would make a good student."

Hardy shook his head. "We put him in school once when he was about ten years old. The school was about a hundred miles from here. We thought it would be just what he needed. You know what that boy did?"

"What?"

"Ran away from that school two nights later, crossed a hundred miles of desert and mountain all by himself. Took him nearly three days and nights, but when he showed up, he looked as calm and happy as if he had just stepped off a bus.

"Now tell me," Hardy went on, "how are you going to keep a boy like that in school? He needs what we've got here in these hills."

Just then a jet plane sped by high in the sky. I gestured up at the plane and the long, white vapor trail it was leaving behind.

"How can these hills answer any of Jim's questions about jet airplanes?" I asked.

After the raft was completed and the machinery was working properly, I spent time taking Jim and his father down for more skin-diving practice. Once we began our search for gold, they would have to be good enough to operate on their own.

We practiced hours and hours with the hose that was attached to the machine on the raft. With the motor on the raft running, this hose would suck up all the loose stone and gravel in the mine. It took two men to hold it and guide it. The loose gravel poured up through the hose and spilled out on the raft, where we could sift through it for gold nuggets.

We had a strict diving schedule—two of us went down while the third rested. That way, no one risked being under water too long. It would have been dangerous to stay down in such cold water. Even short periods of work made us use up energy just in keeping warm. And working with pick and shovel would have been hard enough under any circumstances—let alone a hundred feet under water, held down by lead belts and completely covered over with diving suits.

My only real worry was Jim's age. At sixteen, could he be trusted to do exactly what I told him—nothing more, nothing less?

When I spotted him once, swimming over toward the dangerous shafts, I signaled for him to go to the surface. When we reached the top, I did not wait to get aboard the raft.

"I thought I told you never to go near those old shafts!"

"I just wanted one quick look, Bill," the boy answered.

"Jim," I promised him grimly, "if I catch you near there again, I will keep you from diving altogether."

Jim was not exactly happy about taking orders from me—or from anyone else, for that matter—but he had no choice. When it came to diving, I had the last word. I was boss—and no buts and no ifs!

The work was never easy. It was chop! chop! chop! and dig! dig! dig! hour after hour. We had to work through layers of gravel to get down to the bed rock, where we thought the gold would be. Some days, after an entire day of work, we ended up with only one or two ounces of gold. Some days we ended up with nothing.

But then a day would come when we would find half a dozen giant-size nuggets—worth almost five hundred dollars each in their natural state!

One day Jim and I were working a shaft together. He was bending down and chopping away at a crack between two big rocks. Suddenly I saw him straighten up and signal to me, pointing down into the crack. I looked and saw the gleam of metal. Jim tried to reach in with his hand, but the opening was not big enough.

Now we both worked to make the crack wider. Finally I made the crack wide enough for Jim to put his hand in. He was so excited that a great burst of bubbles came from his tank.

Once we reached the top, Jim opened his fist. In his palm lay a gold coin, the size and like of which I had never seen before.

Gramps came over and examined the coin carefully. He even put it in his mouth and bit it. "This is a Chinese gold coin," he said at last.

"You must be kidding."

"No, I'm not. A great many Chinese spent time in these hills. They came after the first wave of gold miners. Most of them were from California. I remember my daddy talking about them. Wouldn't be surprised if we found more before we get through down there."

"Imagine!" Jim said. "I thought the Chinese were always real calm. But they got the gold fever just like anyone else."

"I know how they must have felt," I thought. The more gold we mined, the more I wanted.

"How did we do today?" I would ask when we were sitting around the camp fire at night.

"Well," Gramps would say, "we got a little."

That was all that counted—to "get a little." I paid hardly any attention to things like the weather. One day was pretty much like the next, anyway. The sun came up early, stayed hot and dry all day, and at night the temperature dropped twenty or thirty degrees, and you shivered under your blankets.

Once in a while we had to suffer through a sand storm. Powerful gusts of wind would blow sheets of sand in to our eyes and mouths, into the cabins and tents, into the machinery on the raft. We carried a taste of sand on our tongues for days afterward!

Gramps always laughed at me. "You think this storm is bad?" he'd say. "Why, you should have seen the sand storms they used to have down in Texas, and El Paso."

Next thing you know, he was telling another of his wild stories:

"This happened a long time ago, when I was riding down through Texas with my daddy. We were following a pack mule, ridden by an Indian guide. Talk about winds! Well, there was a wind blowing then that hadn't let up for three days and three nights. The pack mule was the only one that could follow the trail.

"As we rode along through the hills of sand forming on either side of us, I noticed the pack mule give a kind of jump. Then my daddy stopped short. He and the Indian were looking down at a man's hat sticking up out of the sand. It looked new. My daddy got down on his knees and began to dig it out.

"Well, when he uncovered the hat and made to lift it up, he discovered a man's head inside it. The Indian dropped down and helped my daddy work to scratch the sand out of the man's ears and eyes and mouth. Then the man gave a little cough and said, "Get a shovel. There's a good horse under me!"

Gramps laughed loudly when the story was done. "That, my friend, is what I call a bad sand storm!"

One day Hardy and Gramps went into town. They were going to take our nuggets with them. Some would be sold to bring in enough money to pay our expenses. The rest they would put in the bank. Jim and I stayed behind. He did not feel like going to town and I was glad for a chance to rest.

After Gramps and Hardy drove off, I fished out the book I was reading, picked up a blanket and headed for the shade of the pine trees in the hills.

"Aren't we going to do any diving today?" Jim asked.

"It's going to be a day of rest," I said.

"But I told you about that cave I found yesterday. The place where I pulled out that giant nugget."

"It will be there tomorrow and so will the gold."

Jim frowned. "Let me just go down for a quick look," he pleaded.

I knew how he felt. But I shook my head and said, "Sorry, Jim, but this is a day off."

Suddenly Jim exploded with anger. "You must want to go off and read! You and your stupid books!"

"That's enough, Jim," I said sharply. "If you don't like books, that's your business. You don't have to read them if you don't want to. Just don't try to tell me what *I* should do!"

With that, I wheeled around and walked off. Up in the hills, I lay down and tried to take a nap. But I did not sleep well. The fight had left a bad feeling between Jim and me, and I wanted to straighten it out. I got up and returned to the camp.

As soon as I got near, I realized something was wrong.

It was too quiet. Then I saw that Jim's diving gear was not hanging in its usual place. Had he decided to go down into the mine by himself?

I quickly suited up. I would have to go down and order him up.

I knifed down through the water, heading toward the spot where we had worked yesterday. The water seemed colder than usual. Then I saw him.

He was near the floor of the mine. His arms were moving wildly. It was easy to see that he was very frightened.

I swam over to him and grabbed his hands. The mouth piece had come out of his mouth. No bubbles streamed up from his tank. His air tanks must have run out—but, by good luck, only a moment before I got there.

Quickly I shoved my mouth piece in to his mouth. The air snapped him to. He gave a start and his whole body trembled. His eyes opened, and behind the face mask I could read terror. But I gripped him tightly and started up with him, signaling him to breathe slowly and steadily. As we went up, I passed the mouth piece back and forth from his mouth to mine, reminding him to breathe out in order to pass off the gases in his blood stream.

Finally we reached the surface. I dragged the gasping and frightened boy to the shore and wrapped him in blankets. When he had got his breath back, he said, "I'm sorry, Bill. I know I was wrong to go diving all alone." He shook his head, puzzled. "What happened?"

"One," I told him, "you stayed down too long. Two, you forgot to check your time and your air tanks. And I know why. You were too busy doing something to spite me to remember what I've taught you."

Jim could not look at me. "You are right, Bill," he said. "I wanted to prove that I didn't have to take orders from you. I wanted to stay down longer than you or anybody else could."

"I guess I'm about the first person who ever expected you to take orders, isn't that right? When you ran away from school, did your father make you go back? Of course not! You had your own way. You have had your own way all your life."

Jim grinned sheepishly. He was an honest kid—he could admit the truth to himself.

"Well, that's none of my business," I went on. "But when it comes to diving, I'm in charge. And either you follow my rules, or you don't dive!"

"I'm sorry, Bill," he mumbled. "I just wanted to be like you—brave and all that."

It was a pretty nice thing to hear about yourself from a kid like Jim, but I would not let myself soften. "I'm not brave," I told him flatly. "I just use my head. And in diving, that's the thing that counts."

Jim nodded. "Okay, Bill. I promise. From now on, I do what you tell me."

I was about to say something more when I heard the car coming back again. Hardy drove up quickly and jumped out from behind the wheel. There was a wild look on his face, and I knew that something was wrong—terribly wrong.

Chapter 7

A VISIT FROM THE MAXWELLS

Jim and I hurried over to the car.

By the time we got there, Gramps had jumped out and was shouting wildly: "These two fellows came over and started yelling and arguing. . . ." He was so mad that his words ran together.

"Hold on now, Gramps," I said. "Calm down."

"Calm down?" His face was bright red. "Never heard anything like it. *They are trying to take the mine away from us.*"

"What?"

"That's right, that's right. Those two fellows and their legal papers. . . ." He was off again, shouting his head off.

I turned to Hardy. "What happened?"

"When we got to Hilltown," he said, fighting to keep his voice level, "we went straight to the bank to deposit the gold. The Maxwell brothers were standing just inside the door. We didn't say a word. They watched us deposit the sacks of gold, and then they walked out. We didn't pay them any more mind—we just went ahead and took care of our other business.

"A couple of hours later, as we were loading up the car with the supplies, the Maxwells came back. Nance said he had something important to talk over with us. He said he and Bert had just been going through their father's old papers—"

"It's a lie!" Gramps put in suddenly.

Hardy hushed him with a look, then turned back to me. "Nance said that he's found a deed to this mine, a deed that says they still own it."

"But that's impossible!" I said. "Didn't Gramps say he'd bought this property from their father?"

"Yes, but they claim this is a later deed, one which says their father bought back part of this site from Gramps. Nance claims that all we own is the lake and those mountains over there. He insists the flooded mine belongs to them."

"Well, what's the problem?" I said. "All Gramps has to do is show them the deed to the mine."

"The trouble is," Hardy said, "Gramps can't remember where he put it."

Gramps shook his head. "You know how it is when

71

you move around all the time from one town to another. If you have anything valuable, you rent a safe deposit box in a bank and leave it there. After a few years, you find yourself holding a mess of safe deposit box keys. You never know which key belongs to which box."

Gramps sighed. "I think the deed is in the bank in Sonora. But then again, it might be in Oroville. . . ."

"I have a feeling it's in Sonora," Hardy said.

"Then what are we waiting for?" Jim cried. "Let's go there right now and find out."

I thought it over for a moment. "Why didn't the Maxwells mention the deed until after they saw you bring in all that gold today?"

"They could have been playing it smart all along," Hardy said. "Maybe they've been sitting on the deed, waiting to see what we *would* find. That way we would do the dirty work. If we hadn't found gold, maybe they wouldn't have said anything. But now that we have found it, they are making their move."

"We won't let them take it away from us," Gramps said. "If they show up here, we grab our rifles and drive them out of camp. That's the way to handle people like those Maxwells!"

"Calm down," I told him. "After all, none of us has seen this mysterious deed they're talking about."

"But suppose they show up here tomorrow with it?"

"Then we let them take us to court. And we begin searching for Gramps' original deed."

"Court!" Gramps made it sound like a swear word. "I don't trust courts—not a single one of them."

"But you trust the Maxwells to tell the truth?"

"You have something there," Hardy agreed. "The Maxwells are a greedy pair, no doubt about it. They tried to cheat Bill, and they may be trying to cheat us out of our mine."

"What do you think we should do?" Gramps asked.

"We call their bluff," Hardy decided.

In the morning I went to work on the dredge pump. The motor needed tuning and some new parts put in. While Jim helped me, Hardy went to work patching our wet suits.

"Where did you learn to work on engines?" Jim asked me.

"You'll probably laugh at my answer, Jim, but I learned about them mostly from books."

"Honest?"

I pointed to the big manual, stained with grease, which lay on the floor of my jeep. "I carry that thing wherever I go. It tells how to repair practically every kind of motor there is."

I expected Jim to change the subject, but instead he walked over, picked up the manual, and began to look through it.

"You want to see what it says about the motor?" I asked.

He nodded. I found the right page and began reading out loud. And then I went back to work, following the instructions. Jim watched closely. Pretty soon I had the engine humming quietly and evenly.

"Nice work, Bill," Jim said.

"The credit goes to the book, not me." I said it with a laugh, but I hoped I got the point across.

We walked down to the lake's edge to wash our hands. "Thanks for not saying anything to my father about what happened yesterday," Jim said.

"We all make mistakes, Jim."

He sighed. "There's so much to learn, isn't there?"

"The more you learn, the more you realize how much there is still to learn," I agreed.

Jim did not answer that, but I could see he was thinking about what I had said. He did not make any comment when I got the book I was reading and headed for the shade and a rest after lunch. In fact, he did something unusual. Instead of picking up his rifle or a fishing pole and taking off, he sat down on the running board of the jeep and began going through the pages of the manual.

I spent the rest of the afternoon cleaning and checking our diving gear. I washed out the mouth pieces and hoses with fresh water. Jim watched closely as I started the job of getting the air regulators in order. That is a job best left to one with special training, but up here I had no choice but to do it myself.

After watching me fix two regulators, Jim asked if he

could work on the third. I said yes, and sat back on my heels to watch him. Not only did he do the job quickly, but did it every bit as well as I would have myself.

"Nice going, Jim," I told him.

We finished the day with a swim. After dinner we sat around the camp fire, talking things over. Hardy was still worried, but Gramps seemed to have forgotten about the Maxwells. He brought out his mouth organ and began playing tunes and telling jokes, just as he did every night.

Tonight he sang a song about the tough life the miners lived in the days of '49. It told of the bad food they had to eat, the long hours of back-breaking work, the cold they endured in winter and the fierce heat of summer, and of the sweethearts back home who grew tired of waiting for their return and ended up marrying other men. It was a sad song, a good song.

And then it was time to sleep.

In the morning, just as Hardy and I were suiting up to go down, we heard the sound of an approaching car. Hardy's face turned dead white. Gramps cried, "The Maxwells!"

Jim turned toward his tent. "My rifle!" he exclaimed.

"Wait! Don't get excited," I insisted. "Let's hear what they have to say. Remember, they may be bluffing."

So we waited while the car came closer, until it finally braked to a stop. Nance Maxwell got out from the driver's side. His face looked meaner than ever before. He was

75

wearing a pistol. So was Bert, who followed his brother out of the car.

Seeing them again sent a rush of anger through me. I remembered the fight I had had with them and my night in jail.

"I guess you know why we are here," Nance said.

"Suppose you tell us."

Nance looked at me and laughed. "I don't talk to the hired help."

"Get something straight right off," Hardy told him. "Bryan is a partner in this mine."

"That means he's got one-third of nothing," Bert said.

"Come on, speak your piece, Nance," I said. "What's your story?"

Nance eyed me carefully. "I told Hardy and Gramps. We hold a deed that says we own the flooded mine."

"And you are trying to tell us that you just discovered the deed the day before yesterday?"

"That's right, Bryan. We happened across it while we were looking through some old papers."

"I think you are a liar," I said.

Bert's hand moved toward his gun. "Hold on now," Nance said. He wore a tight smile and was trying to make his voice sound pleasant. "We don't want to stir up any trouble. We want to be friends."

"You call trying to take the mine from us an act of friendship?" snapped Hardy.

Nance kept the smile pasted on his face. "Now who

said anything about trying to take the mine from you?"

"You did—in town."

"That was day before yesterday. Today I'm saying that we want to keep peace between us. We own the mine, but we are going to be generous about it. After all, we are old friends, and there is plenty of gold down there. Enough to satisfy all of us, right?"

He was staring at Hardy now. "I still don't know what you are driving at," said Hardy.

"It's simple. We will let you stay here, even though the mine doesn't really belong to you. We will let you work it with us. Whatever we take out we split 50–50. Fifty for you four, and fifty for me and Bert. . . ."

Gramps had kept quiet, but now he exploded. "What? Why, you scheming thieves, you get 50 per cent of this mine over my dead body!"

I said quickly, "Before we even argue about it, can you produce that new deed, Nance? Can you show me what it actually looks like?"

Nance grinned. "You don't think I'd be fool enough to bring it out here, do you? Suppose you decide to hold us up and take it from us? How could we prove our case in court? The deed is our only evidence."

"I still say you are lying, Nance," I said. "I don't believe there is any such deed."

"That's what I get for trying to be nice," he said. "I wanted to avoid trouble. I wanted to settle this thing between us, without having to bring in the law. But now —well, if you have no intention of being reasonable, why should I try to be? I'm going to pay you back in kind. I'm going to the judge and start a legal action against you. I'm going to take the mine away from you. You had your chance to keep half, but you blew it. Before I get finished with you, you won't have a nugget left to your name!"

With that, Nance nodded at Bert, and they walked quickly to the car. A moment later they drove off.

In silence we watched them drive out of sight. Then Hardy sat down, as if his legs would no longer hold him. He buried his head in his hands. "What a mess!"

"Are they really going to take the mine from us?" Jim demanded.

"I don't know," I said slowly. "I still think they are bluffing, but I can't prove it."

"What do we do, Bill?" Gramps asked.

"Nothing."

"Nothing?" cried Gramps. "But. . . ."

"They still haven't produced the deed," I reminded them. "So far, all they've done is threaten us."

"But Nance said he's going to start legal action against us."

"Let him expose his hand. He may not be holding a single good card!"

"And suppose he's holding aces?"

"Then we will fight him in the courts as best we can. Until then, I think we should keep working as if nothing had happened."

There was a long silence. Three pairs of eyes looked at me out of three faces that wore the same worried frowns. But then Gramps sighed and said, "Bill is right. We have to keep calling their bluff. If they produce their paper, then I will produce mine, and we will fight it out from there."

Chapter 8

THE TWISTER

When we woke the next morning, the sky was very gray. A strong wind came down from the mountains, blowing dust and tumble weed around. Dark clouds were hanging low.

"I don't like it," Gramps said, peering up at the sky.

"Looks like a bad storm coming," I agreed. "I don't think anyone should dive today. Let's spend our time securing the camp."

We began by taking apart all the tents and bundling our things together, covering them with canvas and lashing them down with strong ropes. Then we towed the work raft in and dragged it to a safe place on the beach.

Meanwhile, it grew darker and darker. Then the strong wind died down, and everything grew still.

"It seems to be clearing," I said.

"Don't fool yourself," Gramps warned. "This is the worst sign of all—the lull before the storm."

We worked faster now, lashing down bundles of supplies and storing breakable things in big wooden boxes. It took a long time, for there were lots of little things that needed gathering. The air grew hot and heavy. You could feel it pressing down on you like a blanket. Nothing was moving—no birds flew overhead, no rabbits darted across the brush. Every living thing seemed to have gone into hiding.

"We had better find shelter of our own," said Hardy. He gestured toward the well-built wooden shack standing at the center of the camp.

As we started toward it, the wind began to blow again, rattling the doors and windows of the shack.

Then the blasts came more often—hot as the exhaust of a jet engine. We hurried into the shack, closing all the shutters and bolting the door. Suddenly the wind howled like a wild animal. The shack rocked back and forth.

"I know that howl," Gramps yelled. "It's a twister! Let's get out—it's not safe in here."

He was right. We forced the door open and started to dash toward the caves in the hills—and seconds later, the twister hit with all its might. You could actually see the tube-shaped wind, drawing up dirt and dust into the sky with tremendous force. It lashed out here and there like the tail of some fierce beast. It blew the roof off the shack and sent it flying across the ground.

We were lucky to reach the cave without being blown off our feet. It was all we could do to run without being doubled over by its force. We could see the storm pick up whole trees and huge rocks and send them sailing in to the air like balloons.

"Duck!" Hardy cried as we threw ourselves down on the floor of the cave.

"Hold on!" Gramps warned.

The twister hit the side of the hill straight on. We could feel the earth tremble beneath us. Stones and dirt showered down, as if the whole hill might cave in.

The twister swept on, howling with fury and violence. It was as if nature were angry with us, as if she were determined to show us how weak mortals are. In the face of this display of power and strength, we were little better than ants in a hole. All we could do was burrow deep into the ground and pray for it to be over.

It finished as quickly as it had come. Suddenly the howling wind swept down the valley, heading east. All was quiet. The air was still.

We raised our heads cautiously. It was hard to believe the storm had lasted only minutes. I glanced at the others. We were covered with dust, and each face wore a stunned look.

Gramps in particular looked so funny that I had to laugh. The force of the wind had separated the hairs in his beard and dotted it with dirt and dust and bits of wood.

"Gramps," I said, "you look as if you'd just been attacked by an egg beater."

Gramps shook his head. "That was the worst twister I've ever seen."

"How often do they strike?" I wanted to know.

"Not very often. Maybe once in 25 years."

Jim peered cautiously out of the cave.

"Look, the shack is gone!" he cried.

He was right. The twister had lifted the whole structure right off its foundation and blown it into the lake. We could see it floating there, some 500 yards away.

"Imagine what would have happened to us if we had stayed in there," said Hardy.

"I built that shack myself," Gramps said. "It was a good strong job too, built to take punishment." He shook his head again.

We quickly checked our supplies. Some things had been caught up and sent flying all over the place. Others had luckily escaped the cruel wind. The twister had flipped my jeep over on its side. We heaved it upright. No serious harm showed.

Then I remembered our most important possessions of all. "The diving gear," I cried.

"It's under that bundle," Gramps said, pointing.

Moments later I breathed a sigh of relief. Everything looked all right. "We were lucky," I said. "If the twister had worked the air tanks loose, they might have blown up like bombs."

I spent the next hour checking all the gauges and joints to see whether any other damage had been done, but I could not find anything wrong.

When I had finished, I helped the others restore order to the camp. It was slow, difficult work. We got the raft back in to the lake and picked up whatever was floating around out there—parts of the shack, bits of clothing, boxes of food. Then we went ashore and hunted around for other things that belonged to us. When that was done, we set to work putting up our tents and making a new fire place.

As we worked I said to the others, "When I return to the sea, I will never complain about getting caught in a bad storm again. Very few storms at sea can compare to what we just went through."

"If you go through one more twister, you may never see the sea again," said Gramps with a grin. "It might blow you clear across to the Rocky Mountains."

"The way it nearly blew your beard off?"

"Wonder what you'd look like without a beard," Jim said to Gramps.

"Why, you'd get the surprise of your life," Gramps answered. "You'd see that under all this hair is a 16-year-old boy."

We were back to normal. Lots of hard work, and Gramps making jokes.

We put in a long, back-breaking day. By night we were all too tired to eat anything more than cold beans out of a can. Then we went straight to our tents and fell into bed.

In the morning, the sun shone hot and bright. Everything was so beautiful and peaceful, the twister seemed like a bad dream.

Jim and I suited up and dived down to the mine. Jim kicked on ahead, eager to get to work. Twister or no, the gold was still there. I settled happily into the familiar pattern.

As time went by, I began to feel uneasy about something. I kept looking around, but I could not place what was bothering me. The water was neither colder nor darker than usual. We were working a familiar shaft. What could it be?

More time went by. As I worked away, I began to feel that perhaps for once my sixth sense was sounding a false alarm. Maybe I was only suffering the after-effects of yesterday's big storm.

Suddenly something smacked up against me—a current. What a shock! This was the same current we had dammed up weeks and weeks ago. What was wrong? There must be an under ground spring somewhere back in the mine!

Then there was no time to think. A stream of water struck me with such force that I was knocked against the wall of the shaft. My head hit the rock so hard that I almost passed out.

Fortunately, my mouth piece was not jarred loose. I bit into it hard and struggled to keep from being swept out of the shaft by the swift water. At the same time, I realized what might have happened. Yesterday's twister could have struck the dam and put cracks in it here and there. Overnight the current had begun to push into those cracks, forcing them open, making wider and wider holes, pouring through with increasing force.

By now, the current was rushing madly down the shaft of the mine, like an animal freed from a cage.

I grabbed a rock and clung to it with all my might. It took long minutes for the first rush of water to ease up. But at last it did. I still had to fight to keep from being washed down the length of the shaft, but now I could look around for Jim.

The boy was nowhere in sight. I turned this way, that way, but could not spot him. The current had carried him off!

Down the shaft I swam, tossed about by the current. I looked for Jim and saw nothing but muddy water ahead. Around a corner I went, carried along swiftly. Still no Jim.

At last I caught a glimpse of him. He was about 10 feet ahead, being bounced and tumbled around like a rag doll. He must have been knocked out, for he was not fighting the current at all. He was bumping into rocks and against the walls of the shaft.

As I swam after him as fast as I could, I saw where he was heading. The current was taking him toward the mouth of the maze!

Hard as I tried, I could not reach him before he was flung down into the dark, deadly hole. All I could do was dive down blindly after him, a terrible fear in my heart.

Luckily, I was able to move faster than Jim. My long experience in the water served me well. I kicked and swam with all my strength and caught up with him just in time. Another split second, and Jim might have disappeared into any one of a hundred dark holes.

He had passed out, but was still breathing. I saw with relief that his mouth was clenched tight around his mouth piece.

I started to swim up out of the maze with him, fighting the current with every stroke. It was hard to find my way out. I could only keep going, hoping to find a familiar shaft. I had all I could do to maintain my life-saving hold on Jim. I would not have made it to the top with him if he had not come to life half way up.

Half conscious as he was, he understood that he was in trouble. He found the strength to kick upward, helping himself along. Even so, it took us more precious minutes to make it to the surface.

When we broke water, Jim yanked out his mouth piece. "What happened?" he gasped.

"Wait until we reach shore," I told him.

Once on land, we both sank down, exhausted. The others came running over and dragged us up on to the beach.

"The dam—" I explained still panting. "It must have caved in somewhere—let the current through. Happened yesterday—the twister—"

"Take it easy," said Gramps. He and Hardy helped us out of our gear, and we lay in the sun for a long while, getting our strength back.

Later, as we sat by the fire drinking coffee, Hardy said, "Bill, that's the second member of the Clark family whose life you've saved. It's getting to be a habit." He reached over to touch my shoulder. "Thanks, Bill."

Toward the middle of the afternoon I dived again, this time with Hardy. We swam along the length of the dam to see just where the damage was. We discovered three places where the twister had let the current through. Our good luck—it wouldn't take a big job to patch them up. Just a few well-placed under-water charges would send up enough stones to fill everything in.

Between us, we strung the charges in less than a half hour. Then we left the water, and I set off the charges. They blew right on the button. A quick dive down revealed that the job was a complete success. The current had once more been dammed up.

It was a good feeling to know that diving conditions had returned to normal. But I would have felt better if I could have done something about the maze. Its presence spelled constant danger to us.

Chapter 9

THE MAXWELLS MAKE A MOVE

The twister and then the cracking of our dam had pushed the Clarks' worries about the Maxwells right out of their heads.

"Maybe they heard about the storm—maybe they think it ruined the mine," Jim suggested hopefully.

I did not think so, but there was no point in saying it, so I shrugged. "Maybe. Time will tell. In the meantime we have work to do."

"We sure do," Jim answered, his eyes glowing.

The work was going well. The break in our first dam had opened up new areas, shafts that had been blocked off by cave-ins since before the mine was flooded. In fact, the accident was turning out to be a blessing, because the ore we brought up now was even higher grade than the old.

"It sure is good to see those nuggets pile up," Gramps said, a grin splitting his beard.

We all worked together now, like a well-trained team. Jim was doing a steady, careful job of diving. It was a pleasure to watch him swimming and moving around like an expert. He never took foolish chances any more. He always paid the under-water world the respect it demands.

Even Hardy had improved a great deal. He would never become an expert in diving, but what he lacked in skill, he made up in strength and ability to keep going. I no longer felt anxious when I was on land and they were down below together. They had learned how to handle themselves.

"How rich do you think we are?" Jim asked me one evening, as we looked over the ore we had brought up that day.

"That's hard to tell. Let's not count on anything yet—let's just keep on bringing up the gold."

I did not want them to know that I was worried about the Maxwells. Secrets could not be kept in this part of the country. Nance and Bert must have heard about the twister, about the new shafts we were working. They had more reason than ever for wanting to take the mine away from us.

We found ourselves working longer and longer hours. The water was still cold, but we were becoming used to it, able to stay down for long periods. But finally, there came a day when we were all too tired to do any diving.

We slept right through Gramps' first breakfast call. When he finally did manage to get us up, Hardy went back to bed right after breakfast. I was tempted to do the same, but Jim talked me into going hunting with him.

We went up into the hills, Jim at the wheel of my jeep, in search of rabbit. We both wore high leather boots as protection against rattlesnakes. It was a fine day, clear but not too hot. The sky was a perfect blue, and the air smelled good. We drove as far as we could, then started walking and hunting.

Jim handled a rifle beautifully. Whenever a small bit of white darted out, he would snap his gun up and fire almost instantly. And he rarely missed. In less than an hour he had bagged three rabbits.

"That's real shooting," I said.

"Here," Jim said, handing me the rifle, "give it a try."

I tried to handle the rifle the way he did. There were plenty of rabbits around, but I could not hit one of them. I must have fired a dozen times without coming close.

"Jim," I said with a laugh, "I'm out of my element. "Take this rifle back, before I use up all your bullets."

"You are about as bad at hunting as I was at diving when I first began," Jim said, grinning at me.

"Worse," I admitted. "At least you could swim."

We sat down under some trees and took out our lunch. Jim sat quiet for a while, chewing on a sandwich and staring out across the long valley below us. You could see a great distance from up here.

"We are a long way from anywhere," Jim said finally.

"That's for sure," I agreed.

Jim fell silent again. Then: "What's it like in the cities, Bill?"

I could only say, "What can I tell you? It's completely different from this life."

"Better?"

"You'd have to find that out for yourself."

"I suppose," he agreed. "I've been trying to imagine what it's like there."

"Why don't you go and take a look around some day?"

He smiled and nodded his head toward his rifle. "Would they let me bring that and do some hunting?"

"About the only things people hunt for in cities are jobs and taxis."

Jim laughed and started asking me questions about diving. But I could tell that his mind was still in the city.

Then he said, "I've been looking through that manual of yours. There has sure been a lot of stuff written about machines."

"You reading a book?" I kidded him. "Why, what would your father think?"

"I don't let him see me doing it," Jim answered quite seriously. Then, before I could tease him any further, he stood up and said, "Let's go. I'd better get us some more game, or Gramps will bawl me out."

We started walking again. Jim suddenly reached down and picked up something from beside a rock. "Look at this horned toad," he said, holding it up by one leg. "This little thing likes it hot by day and freezing by night. He's just like me. Wonder how he'd get on if he left these hills?"

Before the afternoon was half over, Jim shot five more rabbits. Then we drove back to camp.

Gramps and Hardy were sitting around the fire. "You came just in time," Gramps said to Jim. "I was about to start making a stew, when the thought struck me: I have nothing to put in this stew but potatoes and carrots. Where's the meat, boy?"

Jim had left the rabbits in the jeep. He said, "Sorry, Gramps, but I couldn't hit a thing today. We will have to eat vegetables tonight."

"Don't say that, boy! I'm so hungry my stomach thinks my throat is cut."

Jim laughed and was just about to tease Gramps some more when he heard the sound of an approaching car.

Gramps turned to look, his face growing dark. "The Maxwells!" he said. "I thought we had seen the last of them!"

"It's trouble, Gramps!" Hardy said. "Jim, keep that rifle handy."

The car came in at a high speed and stopped with a squeal of brakes. Nance and Bert jumped out. There was no one with them, but this visit meant trouble all right. You could tell from the way they walked up to us.

Nance threw a piece of paper down on the table. "Read it!" he snapped.

We all stared down at it. It was printed in fancy letters and carried a lot of stamps that looked official. Hardy picked it up with a look of fear on his face.

"It's the deed to the flooded mine," said Nance. "We decided to let you see it after all."

"I bet you heard something!" Jim burst out. "I bet you wouldn't be coming back if you hadn't heard about our new shafts!"

Nance smiled meanly, but didn't try to deny it. "This is your last chance to come in with us," he said. "Now listen! There is enough gold in the mine to satisfy us all. If you let us have half of the take, we won't cause you any trouble. But if you don't, we will have you arrested for being on our property!"

Hardy was staring down at the deed.

"What does it say?" Gramps asked, his voice shaking.

I saw that Hardy's hands were trembling as he reached out to pick up the paper.

"I can tell you what it says," Bert put in. "It says the mine is ours. That's all there is to it."

"No, I want Hardy to tell me," insisted Gramps.

But Hardy was having a difficult time with the deed. Not only was he a poor reader, but I was sure the fancy printing and legal phrases frightened him. "I don't know," he said. "It looks all right—I mean, it's signed by a government agent, and there's an X by your name, Gramps."

"That's a lie," shouted Gramps. "I never signed this mine over to anyone!"

"Your memory has failed you," Bert said. "That's what happens when a man gets old. He forgets things—important things."

"Blast it," Gramps cried wildly. He made a grab for Jim's rifle, but I put out my hand.

"Let me have a look at that deed," I said. I held out my hand for it.

There was a moment of silence. Nance and Bert stood with their hands touching their pistols. Jim had his rifle ready for action.

"Give it to me," I said to Hardy. He hesitated, then handed it over. I studied the deed closely, taking my time. It looked official, all right. It said just what Bert claimed it did—that Gramps had signed over the flooded mine to Bert and Nance. The government stamps were real, too, as far as I could tell. All in all, it looked like bad news for us . . . except that, back in my mind, a thought kept insisting the Maxwells were liars and cheats.

I shot a quick look at the Clarks. They seemed terrified now. If I did not do something fast, they might give in to the Maxwells and sign over 50 per cent of the mine. Quickly, I held the deed up to the sunlight.

"Look all you want," said Nance. "You won't find anything wrong with the deed."

"No," I said, "there's nothing wrong with the deed— but there is something wrong with this paper."

"Liar!" Bert took a step toward me.

"Look at the water mark," I said to Hardy. "You see, there is the name of the company that made the paper. But government deeds don't have this kind of private water mark. They have a water mark that reads: *Property of U. S. Government Printing Office!*"

Hardy wheeled on Nance. "Then you *are* lying," he yelled. "All you have is a fancy fake deed!"

"I warn you!" shouted Nance. "If you don't sign a paper right now, making us all partners, I will have the sheriff arrest you tonight!"

"No sheriff in the world would arrest a man on the basis of a fake deed," I said.

Nance's mouth was pulled tight. He glared at me with hate in his eyes.

Again there was a long, strained silence. My heart was pounding in my chest. I could hear Nance Maxwell breathing heavily, trying to control himself. His eyes met Bert's, then swung back to me.

Then he said, "All right! If that's the way you want it, that's the way you'll get it! Come on, Bert," he snapped at his brother. "Let's get out of here. We all know where we stand now. We know what we have to do."

They started toward the car. I picked up the deed and yelled, "Here, you forgot something."

For answer, Nance spat back over his shoulder.

Then they were gone, roaring wildly down the dusty road.

"So the deed really wasn't worth anything!" Hardy cried, turning to me.

"God bless you, Bill," said Gramps. "They had me fooled there for a minute, they surely did. They had me really believing that I had somehow signed away the mine."

"It's a good thing you know all about water marks," Jim added. "That deed sure looked real to me."

I started laughing. "I don't know anything about water marks," I said.

"What!" Hardy exclaimed. "We heard you with our own ears. You said clear as anything—"

"I was only putting on an act."

"An act!"

"I had to take a chance, Hardy. I had a feeling they were lying. And so I thought fast and made up that stuff about government water marks."

"Hee-hee-hee!" Gramps cried. "You sure fooled them. Oh, how you fooled them!"

Now Hardy and Jim began laughing and shouting.

"That was quick thinking, Bill—"

"—nice going!"

"Hold on," I said. "I may have fooled them for the time being, but that doesn't mean we can stop worrying about them."

"What do you mean?" Jim asked.

"They've tried to gain control of the mine by using tricks. The tricks have failed, so now my guess is they'll

try something else. We haven't seen the last of the Maxwells yet."

"What do you think they'll do?" Hardy asked.

"I'm not sure," I said slowly. "All I know is—they'll be
back."

"Bill is right," said Gramps. "We are going to have
more trouble with those fellows. Big trouble," he added
bitterly.

Chapter 10

ADVENTURE IN THE CITY

We started standing guard the very next day. Maybe the Maxwells had no real intention of doing us harm, but we could not afford to take chances.

"Hardy, you had better take the early-morning watch," I said. "Jim can relieve you at noon, and I will take over in the evening. In between, I'm afraid the watching is up to Gramps."

"Okay by me, Bill," the old man said with spirit. "It's like the old days. My daddy was always having to keep watch over his claim, for fear some mean chiseler would try to jump it."

"Let me stand guard with you, Bill," Jim said to me. "We don't need anybody watching at noon."

I gave him a look. "The Maxwells promised to take a

noon recess, is that it? Besides, I thought you were going to obey orders from now on."

There were no more protests, so that is how we set it up. It was tiring, having to work and stand guard, too. We had no time off at all, not even during the middle of the day when the heat was at its worst. But the Maxwells were people you had to take seriously.

Our guard post was the top of a small hill beside the camp. The view was great. We could look out over the whole lake and the country around it and the roads that led to the camp.

Meanwhile, the diving went on. We were working now in deep, dark water. Since under-water lights can not be used all the time, we had to get used to the darkness. By the end of two hours our eyes ached, and our heads pounded from the strain.

"Man, give me the fresh air and sunshine!" Hardy gasped as he surfaced one day. But when his turn came again, he went back down without a murmur.

The size of the loads kept increasing, and little by little we came to realize that we were on to a really rich vein. One day, Hardy and I took a little time off to swim along the length of the shaft and explore it.

It narrowed and narrowed until it was not much more than a small black hole filled with whirling water. I hugged the bottom, shining my flash light here and there. There was no room to swing a pick, but with my knife, I worked some rocks loose.

They were very heavy, very high-grade ore. I signaled for Hardy to join me, and we went deeper into the hole, picking up loose nuggets. There was gold everywhere.

Hardy pointed to a vein whose dark hump ran the whole length of the shaft. We both hacked at it. Soon, even in the gloom, we could see a smeary yellow color.

I looked at Hardy. His eyes were wide and excited behind his mask, and he made frantic gestures at me. I could not understand. Finally he signaled that he was going to the surface and that I should follow.

When we broke water, he pulled out his mouth piece and yelled, "The mother lode! We hit the mother lode!"

Jim, on the raft, heard him and began to dance with excitement. I could not blame him. The mother lode was the central layer of gold-bearing ore in a mining region. Other veins might be rich in gold, but the mother lode was priceless. A man whose mine held part of the mother lode was rich for life.

"Boy, oh, boy, we struck it rich!" Jim yelled. "Can I go down and see it—please, Bill? The mother lode—oh, gosh, wait till Gramps hears! He always said this was the richest mine in the county! Can I go down, Bill?"

"Soon enough," I promised. "We will have to blast to get that gold up—never saw anything rooted in the ground so tight."

"I will tell Gramps!" The boy dived off the raft and swam to shore. I saw him disappear in the direction of our guard post.

Hardy and I swam ashore and hurried to the equipment shack to see if we had enough dynamite for such a job. The box contained only a few sticks and caps, not nearly enough to blow apart that huge vein.

"I guess we have to drive to Sonora again to buy what we need," Hardy said.

"I will go this time," I said. "A day in the city will be a nice change. And I need a haircut."

"Can I come with you?" That was Jim. He had run all the way back, and was gasping for breath.

"Am I hearing right?" asked Hardy. "You actually want to visit the city?" He turned to me. "Why, I remember the time you couldn't drag that boy to Sonora with a team of horses."

"It's only a visit," I said. If Hardy kept teasing him, Jim would change his mind.

Jim was not looking at either of us now. He stood with his head down, moving his foot along the ground.

"All right," said Hardy. "If you really want to go, Jim, go ahead. It will do you good, I guess. One look at that noisy, smelly city, and you'll rush right back to these hills and never leave them again."

He grinned and winked at me. "I will go up and relieve Gramps," he went on. "He must be dying to hear all about the big new vein."

An idea came to me. "Tell Gramps that he should come to Sonora with us. While Jim and I get supplies, he can go to all the banks there and see if he can locate the real deed to the mine. We ought to know where it is, in case the Maxwells come again."

"Right!" Hardy agreed. "I will tell him." And he went off to the guard post.

I glanced at Jim. "So now you'll discover whether horned toads can live outside of these hills," I said.

Jim made a sour face. "All I want is to see how the other half lives. The crazy half," he added.

We said good-by to Hardy at seven the next morning. He wore a troubled look.

"Take care of yourself, Jim," he warned. "Make sure you don't get lost. Keep the button fastened on your money pocket."

I smiled to myself. It was only in these wild and lonely hills that a day trip to a small city could take on such importance. From the way Hardy was talking, you would think Jim was leaving for a foreign country.

"Hardy," I said, "don't worry about Jim. You are the one to be careful. Keep a close watch!"

"I will be all right," Hardy assured me. As we climbed into the jeep, he said, "Have a good trip—and don't come back too late."

Just as I started the jeep, Gramps suddenly cried, "Hey, wait a minute!" He jumped out of the jeep and ran to his cabin. A moment later he came back, carrying a huge paper bag filled to the bursting point.

"What's that?" I asked as he climbed back in.

"Why, it's our lunch," he said.

I shook my head as we drove off. "You and your food," I said. "I've never seen anyone eat the way you do."

"If you think I eat a lot, you should see a Tote Road Shagamaw when it's eating."

"Here he goes again," Jim said, shaking his head.

"Laugh all you want, but I've seen this frightening beast."

"What does it look like?" I asked.

"Its hind legs have the hoofs of a moose and its front legs the claws of a bear. When it gets tired of using one set of legs, it travels on the other set. It sneaks along the roads, devouring coats and other articles of miners' clothing which it finds hung on trees or logs. Though it is fierce in appearance, it is shy as a young deer and does no harm!"

All of us laughed, and I said, "Well, Gramps, if I see one along the road, I will be sure to stop and let you capture it."

"You'll never capture it," Gramps said. "It will come to you only if you play 'O Susanna' on the mouth organ."

We arrived in Sonora at noon. In spite of the heat, everyone seemed to be out on the streets. People rushed this way and that, salesmen with their sample cases, women with their arms full of bundles. Traffic was heavy.

I felt a little frightened by it. I had forgotten how noisy cities were, how difficult it was to drive down a main street and look five different ways at once. And, how dusty it smelled, after the clean sweet air of the hills! As I wiped the sweat off my forehead, I saw that my handkerchief already showed dirt.

If the city was affecting me like this, what was it doing to Jim? I turned and glanced at him. His eyes were opened wide, and he looked a little frightened, too. It was all new to him, he hardly knew where to look first. He did not say a word, but his eyes shot here, there, everywhere.

I parked the jeep in a city parking lot.

"Let me start making the rounds of the banks," Gramps said. "You fellows go off and do what you have to do. I will meet you in that café when you are through."

"All right," I agreed. "Are you sure you have all the keys to your various safe deposit boxes with you?"

"I have them all," Gramps assured me. "And now that I'm here, I think I know which bank I put the deed in."

We said good-by, and Jim and I headed down the main street. As we walked along, I noticed Jim staring at a young couple we passed. The boy was about Jim's age. His black hair was carefully cut and combed, and he wore black trousers and a bright sport shirt. He was walking hand in hand with a very pretty girl, who was wearing a light summer dress. Her blond hair bounced up and down as she walked. She looked young and lovely.

The girl and the boy laughed at something together as they walked, and the sound of their laughter lingered after they were gone. Jim stood there staring after them.

"Come on," I said finally. "Let's go shopping."

We went into the shop that sold under-water dynamite. The man who owned the shop was very friendly. He knew my old friend Arnie Lewis, so we talked about him for a while and about the gold rush that was on. Then I bought the things we needed, plus a batch of the latest skin-diving magazines. I needed to know what was happening in my world outside. I bought some other magazines as well, after leaving the store.

Jim still did not say much. But if his mouth was still, his eyes were not. They darted every which way, taking in store windows, the faces of people, the different kinds of cars that went by. He jumped at every sudden noise, such as the sound of a car horn or the squeal of a radio. But as he began to get used to the city, he grew calmer and asked more questions about the things he saw.

"Look at that big glass building," he said, pointing to it. "Doesn't it get terribly hot for the people inside?"

I laughed and said, "You know something, Jim, I've often wondered about that myself. But it's probably air-conditioned. Most new buildings are, these days."

The more places we went, the more questions Jim asked.

In a large market: "Why do people have all their food wrapped?"

"They like it that way, I guess."

"Even meat?"

"Even meat."

He shook his head, and I knew he was thinking of all the game he had shot, and then skinned and cleaned for Gramps to cook. And, probably, how good and fresh it smelled. And I realized myself that city people hardly smelled the food they bought at all, even bread. What a difference from the bread Gramps baked—steaming hot and smelling fresh and good, a smell that immediately made you hungry.

As we shopped around, Jim got a look at many stores he had never been in before—a department store, a big fancy drug store with soda fountains, and others. On setting foot in the department store, he just stopped short and looked in wonder at the huge mounds of goods and at the bright lights and the bustling people.

"Are there enough people in the world to buy all these things?" he asked, shaking his head in surprise.

We finished buying what we needed and locked everything in the jeep. I asked Jim what he wanted to do. "Let's keep walking and looking around," he said.

A short time later, after I had my hair cut, we found ourselves in front of the public library. "Want to have a look in here?" I asked.

He hesitated, so I led the way up the steps. Inside the main reading room, Jim stopped short again at the sight of so many books.

"I know what you are about to ask," I told him with a grin. "Are there enough people in the world to read all these books?"

We wandered quietly through the library. Jim observed the different kinds of people using the reading room, the reference room, the room where newspapers and magazines were in racks—old men, young men, men in business suits, men in cowboy pants and work boots. Then we went upstairs to the children's reading room. We looked around there and stopped at the section containing books on under-water history. I pulled a volume out and turned to a page showing a sketch by the artist Leonardo Da Vinci, made many hundreds of years ago. It was a pair of diving flippers—to be worn on the hands, not the feet. The man diving was supposed to slip them on as he would a pair of gloves.

"When was that drawn?" Jim asked.

"In the 16th century," I said.

"Did the diving men actually use them?"

"I think they tried them out. From hand flippers, some-body then got the idea of foot flippers. The principle is the same. They help you swim faster with less work."

"What kind of diving was done in the 16th century? Did they dive for gold? Did they dive holding their breath or did they take air from above?" The questions shot from Jim's mouth.

"Hold on now," I interrupted, "if you really want all those questions answered, read this book. It's a complete history of diving. It tells almost everything there is to tell about the subject."

"Ah, I couldn't read all those darn words," Jim said.

I pointed out the other boys and girls his age who were sitting and reading various kinds of books. "If they can do it, why can't you?"

That stumped Jim. He turned away and said nothing more.

When we left the library, I asked, "Had enough? Want to go back home?"

"No, not yet!" he answered.

He was soaking up everything now like a sponge, taking in all the sights and sounds and colors and smells of the city. All these new and interesting things had brought an eager look to his eyes.

My feet began to feel as though we had walked down

every block in the city. We roamed from the grounds of the high school out to the city air port. Jim loved it out there. I could hardly tear him away from the observation deck, he was so interested in the planes landing and taking off. He especially liked the jets, which roared up in to the blue sky with a mighty blast. Again, he was full of questions about the jets and the men who flew them.

I tried to answer everything, but in the end could only throw up my hands and say, "Jim, go get yourself a book. You've stumped me."

When we got back to the center of town, I took him into a clothing shop. Hardy had asked me to buy him a couple of new outfits. "I guess you'll be wanting a new pair of blue jeans and some work shirts," I said.

But Jim shook his head. "No, I want something else."

"What?" I asked.

"A pair of black pants and a sport shirt," he said.

I smiled a little to myself, thinking of that lovely young girl in the summer dress and the way Jim had looked at her. But all I said was, "All right, Jim, whatever you say."

Jim insisted on wearing his new clothes. When we entered the café, Gramps' mouth dropped open. "Well, look at you!" he cried. "Look at you stepping along like a rooster in deep mud! What a pretty picture!"

Jim frowned. "Aw, Gramps, haven't you ever seen new clothes before?"

Partly to take the heat off Jim, but mostly because I could not wait another minute to know the answer, I asked, "Well, how about it, Gramps—did you find it?"

The old man nodded, his eyes filled with satisfaction and pride. "I sure did, Bill. I found the deed to the flooded mine, tucked away safe as you please!"

I let out a long whistle. "Man, is that ever a relief! Now we know for sure that nobody can take the mine away from us. Not within the law, anyhow."

As we drove home, I glanced over at Jim—a new Jim, sitting there beside me. It was not only the clothes that made him different, it was Jim himself. The city had changed him. To what extent I could not be sure, and I could not be sure how long this would last, either. But he was not the same boy who left home with us that morning. . . .

Chapter 11

THE ATTACK

When we drove into camp, Hardy came rushing over. "Did you find the deed?"

"Yep!" Gramps said. "But Bill made me put it right back."

"Put it back? Why, what's the idea of that? We may need it when those Maxwells come back."

"If we do, Gramps can always get it out again," I said. "In the meantime, it's safe, and we know for sure we have it."

"Didn't I tell you?" Gramps cried. "Didn't I say the mine was ours by law? I may be old, but I've still got my good sense. I knew I never signed anything over to those Maxwells."

Hardy let out a long, low whistle of relief. Then he

turned to Jim. "Look at you, boy! I hardly recognized you."

Without a word, Jim pushed past him and went to his tent, pulling the flap closed behind him.

"What's the matter with him?" Hardy wanted to know.

"Nothing," I said. "He had a big day in the city, and I suppose he wants to be alone for a while to think about it."

Hardy nodded a little. Then he asked, "Did you get the dynamite?"

"I did," I answered, "but let's talk about it later. Right now all I want to do is have a swim."

Hardy had a simple supper waiting when I had dried off and put on clean clothes. After eating, we sat around the camp fire for a while. Even Gramps was too tired to entertain us with some of his tales. We said good night, and I walked back with Jim to his tent.

"It was a good day, wasn't it?"

"It was a great day," Jim said. "Thanks for taking me and showing me around."

"Any time you want to go again, just let me know," I said.

He gave me a big grin, nodded and said, "I sure will. Good night, Bill."

This time the job of laying the dynamite was not such a difficult one. Not only did I have Jim and Hardy to help me, but there was a smaller area that needed blasting.

We did not have to throw up a dam, only blast apart a vein of gold. The three of us would have put in all the charges in one day, except that Hardy had to relieve Gramps and stand guard.

"You think we still need to worry about the Maxwells?" asked Gramps when he came down to the raft.

"I don't know," I said. "But why take chances?"

Late the next morning, I set off the charges. From the lake's edge we could hear the sound and see the water shoot up. When the water cleared I let Jim and Hardy go down to look around, while I went up the hill to where Gramps was keeping guard. We sat on a log looking out over the lake. It was a beautiful day, with thick clouds moving slowly across the sky and the sun lighting everything up with a warm glow.

"What country," sighed Gramps.

"I sort of get the idea that you like it," I said, grinning.

Gramps laughed. "I not only like it, I love it. All in all, it's been pretty good to me. Here I am, at my age, still pretty fit. And maybe a rich man to boot—someone with a pile of gold to his name."

"I'm glad for you, Gramps," I said. "You deserve any riches these hills have to offer."

"Thanks, Bill," he said. "But it won't be me who really enjoys all this gold. It will be Hardy and Jim. Not that I'm complaining. Heck, I will die happy just knowing the mine is theirs."

Gramps fell silent for a moment. Then he took a

breath and said, "Bill, do you mind if I ask you something?"

"What is it, Gramps?"

"It has to do with what we've just been talking about. I'm worried about Jim."

"How do you mean?"

"Well, ever since he went into the city with you he's been saying to his father that he'd like to spend more time there, maybe even live there." Gramps shook his head. "From what Hardy says, he's talking crazy—about going to school and such."

"You call that crazy?"

"He has a gold mine that will be his one day. What does he need school for?"

"Why don't you ask Jim that question?"

"I will," said Gramps. "All I want to know is whether you put those thoughts in his head."

"Gramps, all I've done is become Jim's friend. Maybe I did put some thoughts in his head, but they are thoughts he'd have come upon one day soon anyway. You must realize it, Gramps—Jim is changing. He's growing up. He's leaving boyhood, becoming a man."

"His father grew to be a man in these hills," said Gramps, "but he never once thought of leaving. What was good enough for me was good enough for him."

"Jim is very much like you and Hardy," I said. "He's strong and brave, and he loves these hills. But he's different from you, too. His world is different from yours.

In your day, only a handful of men lived up here. They searched for gold with pans and picks. Today life isn't that simple. Look at us. Here we are, searching for gold with all kinds of equipment. Life itself is more difficult. Jim is beginning to realize this. His curiosity has been aroused. He has a lot of questions in his mind. He wants the answers to them. Some we can give him, but others he must discover on his own—out in the world beyond the hills."

Gramps said nothing. He sat for a while with a frown on his face, tugging slowly at his beard. In the sky a great cloud passed over the sun, and the shade felt good.

Finally, Gramps gave a deep sigh. "I don't know what to say," he admitted. "I've always taken it for granted that Jim would be just like me. But I see now that he will be his own man. What kind of man, though? That's what I can't figure out."

When Jim and Hardy surfaced, they reported in excited voices that the blasting had been a success. The great vein of stone had been cracked open like a coconut. Each held up a big nugget as proof.

"We will be rich men by the time we clean out this shaft," said Hardy.

"I wish I could go down there with you and see what it looks like," said Gramps. He held a nugget in each hand, grinning broadly. "Feel the weight of them! Like iron."

Having discovered this great vein, though, did not make the work any easier. It was still cold and dark down in the lake, and our backs ached from all the stooping over, our eyes smarted from strain. We settled back in to the old pattern—working in twos, with one man remaining up top to share guard duty with Gramps.

I thought of nothing else but the work at hand. Gramps said nothing more about Jim. As for the boy himself, he worked away quietly and steadily and went hunting and fishing when he could. Yet there was something different about him. He seemed quieter, more thoughtful. He kept to himself more than before.

Then one morning Hardy and I dived down in to the mine together. It was just another work day. We went through the sunny top layer of water and passed to the darker waters of the shaft. Everything was the same as always. The walls of the shaft were the same dark gray. The same fish swam by. My back ached in the same place.

I started chopping away at a crack in the rocks, working toward the nuggets at the bottom. Hardy, wearing his old white sneakers, walked along the bottom to a corner some ten or fifteen feet away. He, too, set to work.

Some minutes later something made me look up. I was surprised to see Jim speeding down toward us, air bubbles shooting up behind him. Anger rushed up in me. He had been told to keep watch this morning!

Then I realized that something was wrong. Jim was gesturing upward, eyes blazing with excitement. I looked up. Two men were diving down at us, kicking furiously. Bert and Nance Maxwell—and each carried a knife, thrust out ahead of him!

Chapter 12

FIGHT TO THE DEATH

There was no time to think. There was only time to get ready to defend myself.

By then Jim had warned Hardy. I saw him grab his pick and turn to face the Maxwells.

It was Nance who came at me. He came swiftly, kicking those big, powerful legs of his. It was all I could do to get out of the way. I dodged just in time to escape his knife. His face was white, his eyes glaring with hate. He turned and came back, kicking out at me in fury with one foot.

The kick sent me tumbling. I scrambled wildly, knowing he might stab me from behind. I was not quite fast enough. His knife caught me on the back of the leg, sending pain through me. Nance cut at me again, but this time I was out of the way. Turning quickly, I cut his knife hand.

He dropped his weapon. Before he could recover it, I grabbed him by the throat and pulled out his mouth piece. Then, leaving him to struggle with it, I turned to look for the others.

I saw Jim fighting with Bert, pounding with his fists and kicking out with his feet. Off to one side was Hardy. He was holding his chest, which was bleeding fast and staining the water red.

I started to swim over to Hardy, but just then Bert got his hands on Jim's harness and pulled the whole thing loose. The mouth piece came out of Jim's mouth and his air tanks fell away toward the bottom.

Jim's eyes filled with terror. He was a hundred feet down with no air to breathe! Jim was helpless—too frightened even to try to defend himself, and Bert was moving toward him with his knife out.

With an effort that made my muscles scream in protest, I threw myself at Bert.

I was almost too late. But at the last second my right flipper caught Bert's arm a glancing blow, just enough to spoil his aim. Bert's knife sliced uselessly through the water, and the terrified boy fell back.

Now I had two men to fight. Nance had recovered his own mouth piece and knife and was coming at me from behind. Paying no attention to Jim, Bert attacked me from the opposite direction.

I shot a quick glance at Hardy. He was still in the same position—holding his hand over his wound, the water around him stained with his blood.

I could do nothing but retreat farther down the shaft. The Maxwells came after me again with their knives.

I dodged them as best I could, but soon they backed me into a corner. One knife could simply not hold off two. Pressing my back to the wall, I waited to see which of the two brothers would strike first.

It was Nance. He dived at me, knife ready. I ducked, expecting to feel Bert's knife sink into my side.

But as I fought Nance, I realized that Bert had not attacked. A quick glance showed me why. Jim had come to my rescue!

He was fighting Bert—and winning! In a flash, I realized what had happened. Jim must have overcome his first moment of fright and remembered one of the first things I had taught him—how to put on his diving gear under water. And now he was back in the fight!

It gave me a tremendous feeling of pride in him—and the pride gave me a new strength as I fought with Nance.

Our knives were forgotten now. We struck out, caught at each other's arms, scraping against the rocky floor of the mine. Nance picked up a rock and tried to crash it against the side of my head. I kicked him hard against the wall. He bounced off, mouth piece coming out for an instant. I dived on top of him. The water was full of blood around us.

Then, as quickly as it had started, the fight was over. Jim managed to wound Bert, who took off in fright, leaving a trail of blood. When Nance saw his brother fleeing, all the fight went out of him, and he swam off after Bert.

Jim and I followed them. They swam through shaft after shaft, now and then shooting back a frightened look to see where we were.

Suddenly they came to a wide black hole, like the waiting mouth of a huge shark. They dived down into it, leaving a great trail of bubbles behind. It was the entrance to the maze—that lower part of the mine where the shafts went in all directions without sense, where I nearly got myself lost one day. Jim started to dive after them, but I held his arm.

"No, no!" I signaled.

I reached for my writing slate to warn him off. But I had lost the slate during the fight. So I signaled again "No!" and gestured to indicate that we must return to Hardy.

We swam back quickly and found him on his side. Each of us took one of his arms, and we started up.

Jim began to kick furiously, but I signaled him to slow down. He pointed to his father's wound, but I made it clear that we would have to go slowly and chance the loss of more blood.

It was agony to go up like this, with Hardy hanging like a dead weight in our arms. To make matters worse, my air tanks were almost empty. The furious fighting had caused us to use up much more than the normal amount.

At last we reached surface. There was Gramps, rifle in hand, staring into the water.

"What happened?" he yelled. "Is Hardy all right?"

"Come and help us!" I called back. The three of us dragged Hardy out of the water and carried him to my tent. I cleaned his wound. It was not as deep as it was long. I bandaged it up carefully. Then we wrapped Hardy in blankets. His face was white.

But a few moments later he stirred and opened his eyes. "What . . . what . . . ?"

"Don't talk," I told him. "You have a pretty bad wound. Jim will go for the doctor."

"What . . . about the Maxwells?" Hardy murmured.

"They dived down into the maze. I'm going after them now. I don't think they can escape by themselves."

Hardy nodded weakly. "Be careful . . . don't risk your life for the likes of them." Then he closed his eyes. He was unconscious again.

I turned to Jim. "Take the jeep and drive to Hilltown for the doctor. Get the sheriff, too."

Jim flew off. "And you, Gramps—watch Hardy. And try to keep an eye on the lake. If the Maxwells come up —well, I guess you can take care of yourself."

He nodded grimly and took his seat by the door of the tent.

I cleaned my own wound, then strapped two fresh tanks of air on my back and caught up two balls of string that

Gramps had left in my tent. Then I ran out to the lake and dived.

I streaked down as fast as I knew how, heading for the entrance to the maze. The Maxwells had probably had a lot more air in their tanks at the end of the fight than we had, but it would not hold out forever. It would take time to find them—even if I *could* find them— and more time to come to the surface safely. The chances of getting them out alive did not look good.

On the other hand, they might not have gone far into the maze at all. They might be waiting down there for me—the two of them, with their knives.

I tried not to think about that.

Here was the mother-lode shaft, where the fight took place. I swam along it cautiously, playing my flash light ahead. No sign of Bert and Nance. There was Hardy's pick axe . . . the heap of nuggets we had collected. . . . And here was the entrance to the maze.

I fastened one end of one ball of string to a rock and left the rock in the shaft. Then, releasing the string a little at a time, I swam down into the dark cave. When one ball ran out, I tied it to the next and unrolled that. Later, by following the string, I could find my way back.

Even using two balls, I could only go a couple of hundred yards from the mother-lode shaft. That was barely enough to allow me to swim a short way in to each of the branching shafts of the maze.

I got to the point where they came together. Swimming into them one by one, I shone my light around and banged on my air tank. Then I waited. But there was no answering bang, no movement. If anyone saw my light or heard the noise, he was keeping quiet.

Then I saw something. As I was exploring the fifth shaft, just where it branched into two smaller holes, my flash light came across a familiar sight. I looked closer. A flipper. It could only belong to one of the Maxwells.

I looked around. But where had they gone from here? It could be either of these two narrow holes. My string would not reach much farther. I slipped into the first one as far as I could go, banged on my tank and waited. Then I tried the other. No answer.

I picked up the flipper. It was black, and there was a rip in one side, as if it had been torn on a sharp rock. I remembered suddenly: Bert had been wearing black flippers—Nance's were green.

A lost flipper was a bad sign. Without it, Bert would be slowed down, and I did not think Nance was the kind to wait around for anybody, even his brother. Unless, of course, they had left it there to draw me on. They had tried to ambush me once before.

I made a sudden decision. For my own peace of mind, I had to be sure. Tying the end of my string to another rock, I pushed my way into one of the branching shafts and swam down it a way. It was narrow and crooked—I scraped my arms on the walls—and finally it came to an end. I had to back out, pushing against the walls, until I could turn around.

I tried the other one. It was much shorter and led into another main up-and-down shaft. I clung there, banging on my tank and moving my light around for a long time, but I saw and heard nothing.

I swam back to the place where I had left the end of my string. "Now what?" I thought.

My watch told me that more than an hour had gone by since the fight. How much air had the Maxwells carried? If they were still under water, it must have run out by now. They might have found their way out of the mine by another shaft—that up-and-down one, perhaps, or some other one I did not know about. It was possible. But, anyway, waiting here was hopeless.

Still, I hated to leave. I returned to the main shaft of the maze, then visited each of its branching arms in turn. But the dark, grim holes showed no signs of life. I was just beginning to wind up my string and head back for the working part of the mine when I saw movement.

No—not a human being. A movement in the rock. A sort of shiver in the wall.

At first I thought my eyes were going bad, but then a chunk of rock worked loose and rolled down the side of the shaft. A moment later, another piece followed.

"*Cave-in!*" I thought.

I turned and swam back toward the main shaft of the maze, following my guiding string. "Don't lose your head

—don't lose your head—" I kept warning myself, but fear was making me clumsy. I tugged too hard. The string snapped off, and the end floated away, pushed by a new current.

That new current scared me more than losing the string. It meant that something was driving the water toward me—something like rocks caving in behind me. This was no small crumbling. The whole mine was going—and there I was, in the deepest part!

Blindly I pushed out, playing my flash light around. Was this the main shaft of the maze, this wide spot? Or was it farther on? Or even behind me by now? Where was that string?

I could feel the water pushing harder now, could hear a faint thunder from far off. Another rock worked loose from the wall beside me, rolled out ahead of me and fell and fell and fell. I watched it, thinking, "I'm trapped down here!"

Then my mind cleared, and common sense took over: If that rock could fall so far, I must be near an up-and-down passage—maybe the main shaft of the maze.

I swam two more strokes—and there was the dangling end of my string, leading upward.

Feet pumping, I went up that maze shaft as fast as a swimmer can go. Here was the other end of my string— I had reached the mother-lode shaft. At least I was no longer lost.

But as I swam along the working shaft, my eye was

caught by that hard hump of metal that ran along the floor—the mother-lode. Was it moving? We had had to blast to get parts of it out. Could it possibly be moving of its own accord?

It *was* moving! The cave-in had reached the main part of the mine already. I could hear it now—and feel it in the violent water. I had only seconds to get out of the mine altogether.

It seemed like thirty years. Here was the end of the mother-lode shaft . . . a cross shaft . . . another working shaft. . . . How many more? In my fear, I could not remember. I just kept racing along, following the route out of habit. Ah, here was the central up-and-down shaft. . . .

I was shooting upward faster than I ought to go, but there was no time for slow surfacing now. One more shaft . . . here it was, and there was the entrance. . . .

Just as I shot out of the mine entrance into the lake, the water around me rocked violently. I was turned upside down, pushed this way and that, rolled over and over, tossed back and forth.

The main part of the mine had fallen in. I had escaped with half a second to spare.

I got myself under control finally and dived down, swimming to the far, deep part of the lake. Even here the water was rough, and I guessed that it would remain like that for quite a while. It might be days before the mine had fallen in entirely and the hillside had settled.

"That's the end of our gold-mining days," I thought, realizing it for the first time. "Poor Gramps!"

It would be hard on the Clarks, but as for me, I was surprised at how little I cared. Being in deadly danger twice in one afternoon had cured me of gold fever.

I moved slowly toward the surface, timing myself. No bad effects from my quick dash upward—another piece of good luck. Here was the surface, still rocking with waves, and there on the shore was a little group of people watching anxiously.

Sighting me, two of them waved their arms and began to dance up and down. One was a boy, the other had a long, gray beard.

Chapter 13

A WARM FAREWELL

"Bill, I thought you were a goner!" Gramps said as I climbed out. "Jim and I thought sure you got caught down below. But they can't kill you, any more than they can kill a Clark, can they? He-he-he!"

"Bill—gee, Bill—" was all Jim could manage.

I took a moment to get my breath. There were two men with Gramps and Jim, one of them the sheriff. The other must be the doctor. Jim had made a quick trip.

"How's Hardy?" I asked when I could talk.

"He's resting," Gramps answered. "He's going to be all right. Doc, here, says the wound wasn't very bad. Now maybe he'd better take a look at you."

I slapped the old man on the shoulder. "I'm all right. But the Maxwells—did you see them come to the surface?"

"Not them. Didn't see a thing till about five minutes ago. Then the water started boiling like a pot on the fire, and we heard a sound like thunder—only coming up from the ground—and then part of the hillside caved in. See, over there."

He pointed. A huge area, nearly an acre of hillside, had sunk down—in some places as deep as ten feet.

"The Maxwells' father did a lot of digging in that mine before it was flooded," Gramps said. "I guess it was only the water that held up some of those shafts as long as this."

I explained what had happened down in the mine, how I had found no trace of Nance and Bert except one flipper. "They must have swum around in that maze until they ran out of air," I finished. "We will never know for sure, now."

The sheriff shook his head. "Those fools! Greed made crazy men out of them."

"You said they were respected citizens," I reminded him.

"They used to be," he answered. "But gold does funny things to men."

"What made them try to kill us?" Jim put in.

"Yes," I said, "did they really think they could get away with it? With us missing, they couldn't possibly have hoped to work the mine. Somebody would have told you to investigate."

"They had no intention of working the mine," said the

sheriff. "I made a quick check before leaving Hilltown. The Maxwells had sold the store and packed their things. They meant to kill you, steal all the gold on hand, and go to Mexico. I found their plane tickets in their baggage. They must have figured that by the time somebody reported you missing, they'd be where nobody could catch up with them."

"And they would have made it, too," said Gramps with spirit, "if it weren't for Jim."

Jim muttered something like, "Heck, I didn't do anything," but his grandfather hushed him.

"I was in my tent," Gramps went on to the sheriff and me, "catching a little nap. Jim was keeping watch from the hill, and he saw the Maxwells coming. They entered the lake from the far side and swam across. It was a lucky thing Jim has a hunter's sharp eyes—I don't think I would have spotted them. Anyway, he let out a yell to wake me up, ran down here and grabbed his gear so he could go down to warn you."

"He got there just in time," I said. "Another few seconds, and the Maxwells would have caught us completely by surprise."

"It must have been some fight," Gramps said, and sighed.

"It was," I agreed. Then I turned to Jim. "Not only did you spot the Maxwells in time, but you handled yourself in the water like a professional. When Bert ripped off your air tanks, I thought you'd lose your head and drown.

But minutes later, there you were, fighting back." I held out my hand. "You are quite a man, Jim Clark."

"It's all your doing, Bill," the boy said. "You taught me everything I know."

"I didn't teach you how to fight like that," I said with a smile.

"He gets his fighting heart from me," Gramps put in. His eyes were twinkling now, and he grinned happily. "Did I ever tell you about the time I fought a Rocky Mountain black bear—?"

"Well," the sheriff said hastily, "the doctor and I had better be getting back to town. You let me know if you find out anything more about the Maxwells."

We agreed, thanked them, and said good-by.

"I don't think we will, though," I said when the doctor and the sheriff had driven off. "I don't think anybody will ever find out anything more about the Maxwells."

We looked out over the lake. It seemed quieter now, although the water was probably still rolling and boiling down below. The clear blue surface was all stirred up and muddy.

"They wanted gold, and they didn't care how they got it," Gramps said. "Now they have all the gold anybody could want."

That reminded me. "Gramps," I said. "I'm afraid the mine can't be worked any more."

"I know, Bill," he said, sighing. "I always told you mining was a funny life, didn't I?" Then he began to laugh his big laugh. "But you and I and Jim and Hardy are still alive, and there is plenty of gold in the bank to keep us in comfort for many a long day—so, you won't find me complaining!"

"Me either!" I agreed.

"Well, then, come on up to camp, and while I'm cooking us some supper, I can finish telling you about the time I fought that bear. . . ."

We three walked up to the camp side by side.

It was three days later, and the time had come for me to say good-by to the Clarks. I did not know how I was going to put it, so I got up a little early and walked down to the lake to think about it.

The surface was smooth and silvery and peaceful in the early morning light. A few birds flew by overhead. The sun was just starting to rise. The air was fresh and clean and sharp. It was hard to believe that only three days before, men had been fighting for their lives down below—and that two had been drowned.

But while I was looking at the lake and the mountains, I was really seeing the sea. I wanted to go back, to smell the salt in the air, to dive in warm water, where there were plants and animals of every color and every kind. That was where I belonged, and there was nothing to keep me here any more.

As I had expected, there was no more sign of the Maxwells. Hardy was pretty well recovered. Jim and I had gone down the day before and looked at the mine. It was sealed off, all right—no hope of working it any more. Besides, after all that had gone on down there, I had lost all desire to hunt for gold.

The good smell of coffee drifted past me. Gramps was up. There were a lot of things I was going to miss. Well, I would tell them at breakfast, that was all I could do.

I returned to camp, hungry for Gramps' cooking, and waited until we were all sitting around with plates of food. Then I told them.

There was a long silence. Then Hardy said, "Can't we talk you into waiting a few more months?"

"I don't think so," I told him. "I've got what I wanted

to get when I came here. Cave-in or no cave-in, I would have been leaving pretty soon. With my share of the gold, I can go home and pay off my debts and buy a small boat. I can get a lot of diving jobs if I own my own boat."

"Stay with us a little while longer," Jim begged.

I shook my head. "I'm sorry, Jim," I said, "but my mind is made up. I'm hungry for the sight and the smell of the sea. I've been away from it too long."

"I understand how you feel," said Hardy. "A man should do the things he loves to do, live where he feels at home."

"Mind you, I've become fond of these hills," I told them. "In a way I hate to leave here."

Hardy nodded. "It's men who always spoil things. Nature stays the same." He took a sip of his coffee. "Now I have something to announce."

"What is that?" I asked him.

"We are going to leave here soon ourselves, Bill."

"What?" I couldn't believe it.

"Lying in bed these last few days has given me a chance to think things over. I've decided that we owe it to Jim to send him to school and let him get a good education. He has a good head on his shoulders, and if he has a chance to go back to school, he might go far in life."

"I never thought I'd hear you say that," I said.

Hardy smiled. "Neither did I. I always took it for granted that what was good enough for me would be good enough for him. But now I know I was wrong. Jim needs other things in life. He needs books to read, and to be with people his own age. And with the money we have from the mine, who knows? Maybe we can set him up in business somewhere."

I turned to Gramps. "Do you agree?" I asked.

"When we last talked about this, I didn't know my own mind," he admitted. "But after thinking it over and discussing it with Hardy, I am of a mind to give him his own head. But don't think we are about to give up this place. Not for one blamed minute! We are still out of door people, we Clarks."

"While school is on," Hardy explained, "we will live in Sonora. We can come here on Saturdays and Sundays and in summer."

Now I looked at Jim. He had been sitting quietly all this time, arms wrapped around his drawn-up knees, staring into the fire. "How do you feel about it?" I asked him.

He frowned. "I don't know, Bill. I'd kind of like to read some of those books we saw in the library in Sonora —but maybe I won't be able to make much sense out of them."

"Don't worry about that, Jim," I said. "You'll take to school just as quickly and easily as you took to diving. And if the books should get you down, well, you can always come up here and get away from them for a while."

"That's right," said Hardy. "Jim feels about this place the way you feel about the sea, Bill."

I finished my coffee and stood up.

"Just remember this," said Hardy. "There will always be a place here for you, too, Bill."

"I might take you up on that one day," I told him. "Anyway, it's good to know that I have three such good friends."

They helped me pack my things. An hour later I stood by the side of my heavily loaded jeep and said good-by to each of them.

"Gramps," I said, shaking his hand, "all I can say is that I hope I have half your spirit when I'm your age. You are the most lively, most marvelous old man I have ever met in my life."

He pumped my hand and grinned. "And when you come back, I will be twice as lively. I'm like a piece of good cheese. I get better with age."

After Hardy and I shook hands, he said, "Bill, I will be grateful to you all my life. You've done so much for us that I can't even begin to thank you."

"And I'm grateful to you," I answered. "You have shown me how to be a brave man and a good father. If I ever have a son, I will try to bring him up to be as brave and fine as Jim."

Then it was time to say a last word to the boy. We took a short walk together.

"I've been thinking," Jim said. "I believe I'd like to be a skin diver one day. I'd like to be able to join you and work with you."

"What about these hills?"

"I could live here part of the year and spend the rest with you, couldn't I?"

"Sure you could," I said. "But let's not worry about that now. You need to go to school first, to meet people and soak up all kinds of learning. We will write to each other. And if, when you are done with your education, you want to join me—well, that will be fine with me."

"Thanks, Bill."

"Good-by, Jim," I said.

"Good-by, Bill."

Just then a small horned toad hopped across our path.

"Look at him," Jim said. "He's in a hurry."

"We never did find out whether those things can live in a city."

"I will write and let you know," said Jim, with a little smile.

Minutes later I was in my jeep and heading up the hill. When I had reached the point above camp, I stopped and looked down.

The three Clarks were standing together, waving and calling a warm farewell. "Come back soon, Bill! Come back soon!"

I waved down at them. It was good seeing them like that, framed against the brown hills, bathed in bright, warm sunshine. Behind them the lake looked smooth and cool. High above, an eagle made big, lazy circles in the sky.

"Good-by, Gramps! Good-by, Hardy! Good-by, Jim!"

My voice carried far across the lake and echoed back from the hills.

Then I put the jeep in gear and turned east. As I drove toward the future and my next adventure, I felt my heart beating with excitement and pleasure. I was heading home. I was heading toward the sea.